BAD
ASS
(ish)

BAD ASS

(ish)

JAYMIE HEILMAN

RONSDALE PRESS

BADASS(ISH)
Copyright © 2023 Jaymie Heilman

RONSDALE PRESS
125A – 1030 Denman Street, Vancouver, B.C. Canada V6G 2M6
www.ronsdalepress.com

Interior design by David Lester. Text set in Goudy 11 pt on 16
Cover illustration and design by David Lester

Ronsdale Press wishes to thank the following for their support of its publishing program: the Canada Council for the Arts, the Government of Canada, the British Columbia Arts Council, and the Province of British Columbia through the British Columbia Book Publishing Tax Credit program.

Library and Archives Canada Cataloguing in Publication

Title: Badass(ish) / Jaymie Heilman.
Other titles: Bad ass (ish)
Names: Heilman, Jaymie Patricia, author.
Identifiers: Canadiana (print) 20230468136 | Canadiana (ebook) 20230468144 | ISBN 9781553806899 (softcover) | ISBN 9781553806905 (EPUB) | ISBN 9781553806912 (PDF)
    Subjects: LCGFT: Novels.
Classification: LCC PS8615.E335 B33 2023 | DDC jC813/.6—dc23

Printed in Canada

For AC and AC,
badass sobrinas

PROLOGUE

I can do this.

I most definitely can do this.

Okay, fine. I absolutely cannot do this, but I'll do it anyway. I take the last few steps toward the roof's edge. As long as I don't look down, I'll be fine. As long as I don't trip and stumble and fall eight storeys to the ground, crashing to a very messy death, I'll be fine.

Sirens are shrieking in the distance, and someone is banging on the door and yelling. I don't know how much longer Renzi will be able to hold it shut.

Jae is down on the sidewalk with the video camera, and there must be a hundred people beside her: protestors holding cardboard tombstones and counter-demonstrators with signs of their own. Izzy is there too. He's got a megaphone in his hands, and he's never looked more gorgeous — those wild curls, those massive sideburns and his favourite pink shirt. It's been two long months since he dumped me. Broke my heart and stomped all over it. If anything is going to prove he was wrong about me, it's this.

I double-check that the bungee cords connecting the banner to the roof are secure and get my feet into position. I lift the heavy banner up and then hurl it into the air. It flies out and unfurls, showing our demands to the world.

Izzy throws his fist above his head and whoops.

He lifts the megaphone to his mouth and shouts Renzi's name. And then he hollers three short words that destroy everything.

Two months earlier.

DAVIS

Seven hours and five minutes before Valentine's Day, Izzy pulls away from our half-hearted kiss. I am giving this embrace everything I have, but Izzy seems lost somewhere south of Antarctica.

"This isn't working," he says, leaning against his kitchen counter. He could mean the location because the kitchen tiles are too cold against our feet. He could mean my breath, or the fact that our noses keep crashing together.

But I know that's not what he means. I'm losing him. The one person who likes me *because* of what I did after the Fort Mac fire. The funniest, smartest, most gorgeous guy I've ever met. The only guy I've ever kissed. And I'm losing him.

He looks down at the floor. "Davis, I've been thinking things through. Trying to be honest with myself about what I feel. And I know that what I need is —"

"Vietnamese food!"

His mom's shout from the back door catches us both by surprise. His parents aren't supposed to be home for another

5

few hours. Crap, crap, crap. I have about two seconds to wipe off my smeared lipstick and fix my mussed ponytail.

"We decided to get takeout," Izzy's mom says, coming into the kitchen with Izzy's dad. "Izzy? Set the — oh, hello." Her surprise is obvious. "I'm Sandra."

Whoa. She's way older than I expected. But I guess that makes sense, given that Izzy's sister is old enough to be a doctor. Still, it's kind of weird. Her hair is whiter than my grandma's.

"Styrofoam, Mom? And plastic bags? Plastic forks?! Seriously?" Izzy pulls white boxes of food out of the bags, sounding like he's on the verge of tears. But at least his despair over all the plastic spares me from whatever he was going to declare about our relationship.

"And you are?" Izzy's mom asks, ignoring her son as she pulls out a chair for me. I guess I'm staying for supper.

"Davis," I answer as I sit down, my voice a squeak.

"You know none of this can be recycled, right?" Izzy continues. "It's just gonna sit in some landfill for six hundred years."

I want to slide off my chair, slink down to the floor and then crawl out the front door. To escape. I lower my hand under the table and pinch the side of my thigh as hard as I can, desperately hoping that the pain will calm me down.

(Spoiler alert: it doesn't.)

"They're just takeout containers," Izzy's dad says. He looks at me and rolls his eyes dramatically, like I'm on his side. He waggles his plastic fork at Izzy and says, "You sound exactly like your sister, you know. She was on the radio again today, arguing against the new pipeline."

Yeah, that new pipeline. The one my parents are designing. I cannot let Izzy find that out.

Izzy's dad shakes his head, scooping a bunch of lemongrass beef onto his plate and then passing me the container. "Tar sands this, tar sands that. We spent all that money putting her through med school, and she still hasn't figured out that they're called the oil sands?"

Okay. If I concentrate hard enough, maybe I can make myself invisible and sneak out, and no one will even notice. I reach into my pocket to get my phone so I can text Mom and ask her to come and get me immediately.

But then a hand on mine. Izzy's. The warm current of electricity lightens me, fills me. Maybe he wasn't about to break up with me. Maybe when he said, "I need . . ." all he needed was to go pee. Or study. Or floss. Maybe. Izzy squeezes my hand and looks into my eyes, his gaze so warm, so soft. He smiles, the gentle smile that always melts me. I've been crazily in love with him since I met him in the fall, and the almost two months that we've been together have been amazing. I'd do anything for this guy. Anything at all.

"Davis, here, can tell you all about the Fort Mac tar sands."

Anything at all, except for that.

Everyone's eyes turn to me. Izzy's dad lowers his fork from his mouth. Izzy's mom folds her hands, her lips pressed tightly together.

I know exactly what Izzy wants me to say, the statistics and facts he wants me to rattle off. It's all environmental stuff I feel super passionate about. But I can't. I just can't. I don't know Izzy's parents at all. What if they're like all those angry Albertans who accused me of kicking Fort Mac when

7

it was down? Angry Albertans like my very favourite cousin. It was hard enough enduring that kind of stuff when I was alone with my phone — there's no way I can face that kind of rage in the middle of this already super-awkward dinner. I shove a huge forkful of lemongrass beef into my mouth, even though I've been a vegetarian since I was ten and learned that cow burps heat up our planet. I chew and chew until it's a liquefied mess that will ooze out the sides of my mouth if I don't gulp it down this instant.

I swallow. Sadly, I don't immediately choke and pass out. Everyone is still looking at me, waiting. I give them the shortest possible answer. "My parents and I had to leave Fort McMurray because of the fire," I say quietly. "It killed Porkchop, our golden lab. And this food is delicious, by the way. Super yummy. Where did you get it?"

Way to go, Davis. Way. To. Go. Izzy gave you a test, a last chance. And you blew it. Big time.

When the world's cringiest dinner finally ends, Izzy follows me out to the front porch to wait for my mom. Izzy plops himself down on the porch swing, taking up the entire seat. Should I try to sit there too? Keep standing? I move to sit down and then take a step back, cross my arms and then uncross them.

"I'm sorry, Davis," he says, putting his face in his hands. "I can't do this. It's not you, it's me. I keep wanting you to be someone you're not and —" he lets out a long, shaky sigh — "I love that you wrote that tweet blaming climate change for killing your dog, shaming oil companies and the tar sands, and that you faced down all that rage and hate. I mean, the stuff that happened to you at school last year?

8

That was hardcore. All because of your badass tweet. I love the Davis who wrote that, but you —"

My mom pulls up in our SUV and honks.

Saved by a honk. I run down the steps before Izzy can say anything else. I still have a chance to get him back. I mean, he used the words "I," "love," "you" and "Davis" in a sentence about me. Me. Right? Technically.

But this is not the time for technicalities. This is the time for complete emotional collapse.

And GO.

RENZI

Renzi really wants to ignore the banging on her door, to just remain locked inside the elegant world of linear functions, tangents and secant lines where all the answers are either right or wrong. But the longer she stays silent, the louder her older brother knocks.

"Renzita! Some *papito* brought something for you," Lino yells. "He's on the steps outside." Renzi slams her math book shut and stomps across her bedroom to open her door. Her brother grins and hands her a thick red envelope. "He didn't want to come in, but I told him to wait five minutes while I delivered his very early valentine. That one is too cute to send away."

Renzi groans. It must be the *Zángano* — the fool. Lino crosses his arms and taps his foot, waiting for Renzi to open the envelope. The instant she does, a thick stack of twenties pops out. There's a note too. "For the generator. This is all I have right now, but I can get you more as soon as I get paid." And then a heart with his name.

Caramba. This is all her fault. Renzi had blocked the Zángano's number over Christmas, but she hadn't removed him from her Instagram account. He must have seen the picture of the solar-powered generator she'd posted. Her grandparents have been relying on a stinky diesel generator since the twin hurricanes hit Puerto Rico in September, but this solar one costs $2,500 more than Renzi has.

Lino lets out a low whistle. "He's gorgeous AND rich, Renzi Chan Cruz. Go!"

Renzi hurries to pull on her parka and boots, hating how conflicted she feels. Good thing Jae has gone home already. If she'd been here when the Zángano showed up, things would have turned awkward, fast. But still, the money for the generator is amazing. It will finally let Renzi help her grandparents — her *abuelos* — for real. Renzi knows her mom is doing everything she can to send as much money as possible to them each month. *Mami* hasn't called an electrician to fix the broken outlet upstairs, she's been taking the train to her office at the university instead of driving, and she hasn't bought a single pair of new shoes in ages. That last one alone is overwhelming proof that her mom is making major financial sacrifices to help their family in Puerto Rico.

Renzi opens the door and steps outside. She sits down beside Izzy on her front steps and takes his hand in hers, in a totally "just friends" kind of way. It's freezing out, but she doesn't invite him into her townhouse. She's told him over and over that she really just wants to be single. She can't let him inside, even though he is a hottie. Even though he's the only person who sees the connection between this stupid new pipeline project and the hurricanes that decimated Puerto

11

Rico. Letting him inside the house would be too confusing for him — and maybe even for her.

"Gracias," she says, kissing him on the cheek. Because that's what Islanders do. They kiss on the cheek — to say hello, to say goodbye, to say thank you — and that is all this kiss means. And if the Zángano misunderstands, misreads what she's doing, that isn't really her fault. Letting him kiss her on the mouth and pull her body tightly against his: that is her fault.

The guilt comes crashing in, and Renzi pulls away. She knows Izzy has a girlfriend, just like she knows kissing Izzy is a betrayal of her very best friend, Jae, who makes barfing noises every time she even sees Izzy. Still, it isn't easy to break away from Izzy's embrace. Renzi hasn't kissed anyone since she broke up with Camilo in the summer, and making out with the Zángano is even nicer, sweeter, than she had imagined it would be. A bit sloppier too. "Izzy, I know you're with that Davis girl," she says. She stands up, knowing that she has to make Izzy leave before this goes any further.

"Who?" the Zángano replies. He stands up, too, and leans in for another kiss. Renzi steps back and Izzy stumbles forward, but Renzi chooses not to catch him. "You have a girlfriend. I'm not —"

"I mostly broke up with her," Izzy rushes to say.

"Mostly?" Renzi raises both eyebrows. "What the actual hell does that even mean?"

"You know how I feel about you, and Davis is just way too nee—" Renzi puts out her hands, fingers stretched to the pitch-black sky. Stop. Stop right there. The temperature outside plummets. It might be the cold wind picking up. Or it

12

might be the ice daggers shooting from her eyeballs because Izzy almost called his girlfriend needy.

"Too needing of time and space. And the chance to be on her own," Izzy continues. He smiles sadly and sighs. "Davis has gone through so much, and I think she needs to take the time to see how strong she really is. To see that she can stand on her own without a guy complicating things, you know?"

Right. But Renzi did know. She'd told Izzy essentially the same thing about herself when he asked her out at Halloween, and again in November and again right after the Christmas break. She completely hates that she's so attracted to him, so drawn to him, but at least his persistence never quite crosses the line from frustrating to creepy.

"I don't want to pressure you," Izzy says, shoving his hands in his pockets. "I respect you way too much to do that. But when you're ready, Renz, I'm here."

Oh, God. Not these same lines again. Sometimes Renzi wonders if Izzy has convinced himself he is in love with her solely because she refuses to date him. She walks to her front door to let herself back inside, but the Zángano doesn't take the hint. He's too busy texting.

"There. Done," he says, holding out his phone for Renzi to see. There is a long string of texts from Davis, followed by three that the Zángano just sent.

Izzy: I need some time alone

Izzy: I need to end things between us

Izzy: You're better off without me

Renzi doesn't bother to stifle her groan. She's reminded again of why she calls Izzy the Zángano. The fool.

JAE

The night air is brutally cold and Jae's belly is uncomfortably full, but the pain is worth it. Renzi's mom had made a vegan sancocho just for her, Puerto Rican beef stew without the beef. The food was amazing, but it wasn't even close to the best part of eating at Renzi's house. The bright orange tablecloth and the fuchsia walls, the salsa music playing while they laughed and talked, and the questions and hugs and genuine interest in Jae's thoughts and ideas — all of that was so radically unlike the sterile silence of Jae's McMansion. And her hermetically sealed mother. Jae eats with Renzi, Lino and their mom, Marisol, at least once a week. She wishes it were more often.

But she doesn't want to push it.

In a weird sort of way, she misses those eleven scary and horrible days of sleeping on Renzi's floor right after the hurricanes hit in September as they waited for news about Renzi's family in Puerto Rico. Renzi, Lino and Marisol were like zombies for that stretch of time, so Jae moved in temporarily to make sure they remembered to eat. And even though it was such a devastating time, it was also incredibly special. For Jae, at least. Probably only for her.

The whole time, Jae half-expected her mother to insist she come home. To demand it. But her mother hadn't. She barely even checked in with Jae. There was a big deadline at her mother's work that week, which no doubt explained why she had been so quick to allow Jae's extended stay away. Only Jennylyn, the Filipina woman who'd been Jae's nanny and who still did all the cooking and cleaning and grocery shopping for Jae and her mother, expressed concern. Only Jennylyn texted constantly. Only Jennylyn urged Jae to make sure Renzi's mom was okay with Jae staying there.

And Marisol was. "But thank you for asking, Jae, *querida*," she had said. "Renzi needs her best friend right now, and having my second daughter around helps me too."

Her second daughter. Words that still wrap around Jae like a big, warm hug. Nothing will change when Jae tells Renzi the full truth about herself, right? The environmental crimes of oil tycoons, the cruelty of a society with a 1%, the scourge of extreme inequality on society — those are all regular topics of conversation at Renzi's dinner table. What will happen when Jae reveals that she's super rich and that her mother defends Haus Oil and its billionaire owners for a living? Will there be some new, subtle awkwardness on Renzi's part when they talk about social justice or environmental stuff? Will Marisol balk at Jae coming over constantly, or even just hesitate a little if Renzi invites Jae to stay for dinner? Of course that won't happen. It's unfair to even imagine it might. But Jae's imagination goes there, anyways. Her friendship with

Renzi, her place inside Renzi's family and world, all of that matters more to Jae than anything.

Crossing bells start clanging as Jae makes the long, cold trek home from Renzi's. The February wind bites at her face, and she can't pull her scarf any higher or her glasses will fog up. What's the Spanish expression . . . *Qué frío?* She should know by now. When Jae met Renzi, in grade eleven, Renzi almost never used Spanish words. But since September, every third word out of Renzi's mouth is Spanish.

Jae probably should have driven, but the longer she can stay away from her house, the happier she is. Besides, as frigid as it is outside, it's still warmer and more welcoming than her own house. The freight train chugs by, and as it passes, Jae hears something.

Something bad.

She runs toward the tracks, following the sound, and even though it's pretty dark out, Jae sees the coyote right away. Bigger than a dog and smaller than a wolf, the coyote is lying on its side. She takes a few steps toward it, but then she stops herself. She knows how dangerous the animal can be, how powerful. Even Jae has limits.

She grabs her phone, pulling off her thick mitten to press the right button and turn it into a flashlight.

The coyote's alive.

She thinks.

Jae switches off the flashlight and presses 9 and 1, but then stops. Paramedics aren't going to rush to the scene for a wounded coyote. She does a quick search and then dials another number, hoping her hand won't get too frostbitten.

"Wild Earth Animal Rescue, Kat speaking."

Jae blubbers out an explanation of what happened and where she is, and the girl on the phone says someone will come right away.

Jae wraps her arms around herself and jumps up and down to keep warm, keeping her eyes on the injured animal. The phone gives off just enough light to let Jae see that the coyote's chest is still moving, the steady up and down of breathing. Its pointy ears twitch a bit, and its black-tufted tail moves slightly, but the coyote remains on its side.

Trains suck. Jae can't ever tell this to Renzi, because Renzi keeps saying this new pipeline is going to make climate change worse, and Jae DEFINITELY would not say this to her own mother, who works for Haus Oil, but Jae knows the Haus pipeline would have some benefits. If they don't build the pipeline, they'll just send more and more oil by train. Premier Nancy Reese has already said so. And more trains will mean more and more injured animals. Dead animals. Moose. Coyotes. Deer. Probably birds too.

And then there was that explosion and fire in Quebec a few years back, when a train carrying oil derailed. So many animals killed.

And so many people too.

Jae hears the truck before she sees it. She turns and sees a girl jumping out of the driver's seat and slamming the truck's door. The girl had killed the engine but left the truck's headlights on. The slammed door did it: the coyote lifts its head and slowly, shakily gets to its feet.

The girl waves her arms and shouts, "Go on! Git! Scram!" She doesn't seem frightened or angry or worried. Just confident. Knowledgeable.

The coyote starts walking, like it's drunk and dazed. The truck's headlights wash the area in light, and Jae can see there's no blood on the ground.

"Go on! Go!" The girl claps her hands over her head. Out of the side of her mouth, she says, "I could use some help here. We need to scare it to make sure it's okay."

Jae snaps into action. She doesn't have time to feel embarrassed about how she could and should have done this on her own. She raises her hands too, clapping and shouting. "Go! Go! Go!"

The coyote turns and looks at the shouting girls, and then it runs. Racing away like nothing had happened.

"That was easy," the girl laughs. "I can tell by the way he's running that he wasn't really injured. Just stunned. You did the right thing by calling, though."

"Woo hoo!" Jae whoops with relief. She's so happy, so relieved, that she immediately throws her arms around the girl, who's now beside her, realizing just a fraction of a second too late that it's weird to hug a total stranger.

"Sorry, I —" Jae says, mortified. Her mother always criticizes her for being too quick to hug, too touchy, too feely. But the girl just smiles. The glow from the truck's headlights lets Jae take a close look. The girl's a lot taller than Jae, thin and wiry, with spiky brown hair and a cute little gap between her front teeth. Probably a bit older too. Maybe. Sometimes it's hard to tell.

"Don't apologize," the girl says. Her parka's open and Jae sees that she has a little whale tattoo on her collarbone. Would that have hurt? Jae looks away, suddenly worried that she was staring at it too long.

"I'm Kat, by the way."

"Your name's Kat, and you work for an animal rescue." Jae groans at her own joke. "I'm sure you've never heard that one before. I'm Jae."

The girl grins. She has the biggest, most amazing smile Jae has ever seen. And a big dimple on her right cheek. "Your name's Jae, and you called animal rescue for an animal most people hate."

"We're totally alike," Jae says. She feels the heat in her cheeks, despite the frigid air. Like she's blushing.

The girl tilts her head. Her grin is now a small smile, but it's still warm, friendly. "I really hope so."

DAVIS

A garbled robot sound announces the arrival of a text. Maybe it's Izzy finally responding to one of the eighty thousand texts I've sent him since he dumped me.

Maybe it's my cousin Carly finally unghosting me.

Ben: Did u see the new Intergalactic episode last night?
Davis: Nope. Was over at Izzy's. We broke up.
Ben: U finally dumped Mr. Wonderful?!?

Ben's never been a fan. Izzy's probably the only thing Ben and I disagree about. But I know Ben knows that I was not the dumper.

Ben: U ok?
Davis: Nope.
Ben: U know that E & E are gonna swoop in and make
   u binge-watch rom-coms or something, right? 😫

Frack. He's right. Ugh. It's horrible to admit it, but one of the best parts about dating Izzy was that it gave me a totally legit excuse for avoiding Ella and Emma and their constant reminders that they rescue-adopted me last May when I showed up after fleeing the Fort Mac fire.

> Davis: Way, way worse than rom-coms.
> Davis: Hockey highlight reels.
> Ben: 😨

Ben Cron — the one and only friend I can reliably count on to make me laugh. Actually, the one and only real friend I have. I barely hear from any of my Fort Mac friends, probably because of my post-fire tweet, and I'm not sure I really consider Ella and Emma my friends. Life would be a lot easier if I could be crazily in love with Ben instead of Izzy. But no such luck. I fling myself back on my bed and stare at my empty light-blue walls. Back in Fort Mac, I plastered my room with retro sci-fi posters. *Alien. Blade Runner. Metropolis. The Thing.* I loved those posters. And they all burned to a crisp, so I've just left my new walls blank.

"Knock, knock." Dad always makes a point of announcing his knocks on my bedroom door, even when it's wide open. The habit is just as much to invite a "Who's there?" joke as it is to ensure that he doesn't accidentally see me in my underwear.

"You going to be okay, kiddo?" Dad asks. He's got his coat and toque on and his suitcase beside him. With all the breakup drama, I'd forgotten that this was his fly-out-to-Fort-McMurray-day. The tar sands mean that even engineers have to spend half of each month away from their families, and I know he hates that as much as Mom and I do.

"I've survived worse," I say, giving him a long hug. I don't want to worry him. "You're still looking for another job, right? In wind power? Or solar? Something other than tar or pipelines? Something where you can stay here with Mom and me, right?"

He kisses me on the head. "You betcha," he says and then hustles away. We've had this conversation about eighty billion times, and he usually ends it by suggesting he plant a big old money tree in our backyard.

"Davis!" Mom calls from downstairs a half hour later. "Time to go!"

It's Valentine's Day, and there is no way in hell I'm going to school today. Hot tears spill from my eyes, and I wipe them away, trying not to think about how Porkchop would have licked them off my face. I don't want to think about Porkchop, so I pull out my phone and look for the seven hundredth time at the texts Izzy sent me late last night.

Just in case I somehow misinterpreted them.

Mom isn't going to let me skip class. (I asked. Twice.) So I just accept her ride to school, walk in through the front doors and then head straight toward the back exit.

I pull the Valentine's card I made for Izzy from my backpack and chuck it into the recycling bin as I pass through the hallway. I worked so hard on it, looking for the funniest, goofiest memes I could. In the end, I printed, cut, coloured and glued one that showed the silhouette of a girl sitting on the planet with the words "My love for you is like climate change" on the front and "It cannot be denied" written on the inside.

I thought the card was dorky and cute. Adorkable. I'd hoped it would take our relationship to a new level of closeness by throwing in the big L-word. I even looked up the address of the closest birth control clinic, readying myself to take that step with Izzy.

I'm such a total and complete jackass.

I really don't understand what happened. What changed between us? I thought we were happy. I thought things were going well. Or well-ish. Medium-well. It's not like Izzy was ever as into me as I was into him, but I still didn't see this breakup coming.

"Davis!"

Two sweet voices call my name in unison, and I picture them before I turn around: cute black leggings, pink hoodies and matching messy buns.

"You are SO coming over to watch the game tonight," Ella says as I turn around.

"No excuses this time," Emma adds.

I was wrong. They aren't wearing pink hoodies; they're wearing matching Oilers jerseys. Ella reaches into her backpack and hands me something: a third matching jersey, wrapped in a red bow.

"It's my old one," she explains.

They position themselves in front of me, and I have no choice but to say something. A normal person would just lie and escape, but I'm so exhausted and edgy that my mouth just starts talking as I shove the jersey into my backpack.

"It's messed up how everything in this province is tangled up with oil. Our hockey team is named after oil. People work for oil companies, or their parents or cousins or friends' parents and cousins do. Including mine. Highways are filled with —"

"Shhh," Emma says.

"Volume, Davis. Volume." Ella motions downward with her hands. "Please don't go into shit-disturber mode this early in the morning."

I haven't talked about oil to anyone other than Izzy and my parents since last May, but here I am. Maybe because I don't care what these two think, or maybe it's because I actually *want* to alienate them.

"Sometimes shit-disturber mode just sort of happens to me. One minute, there's a big old doody on the sidewalk. The next second, it's all over my feet, getting tracked everywhere and smeared on everything."

"Eww."

"Gross. Also, didn't Ella and I totally have to mop you up after you went into shit-disturber mode last year? Maybe you should try to remember that."

As if I could ever, ever forget. I stuff my hand in my pocket and pinch my leg, hard. I check my phone. No new texts from Izzy, but Emma and Ella won't know if I lie. I hold my phone up and say, "Urgent Valentine's Day business." And then I run past them for the school's exit.

The cold air slaps my face as I exit the school. I pull my parka tight around my body, wishing I'd remembered to wear a scarf, and I walk as quickly as I can to the End of the World. It's this lookout place by the river. There used to be a road here, but all that's left now is a portion of its concrete foundation, covered in graffiti and decorated with used condoms and crushed beer cans.

I ran into Izzy here after school on the first day back after Christmas break. I had maybe, sort of, kind of followed him here. The way I had maybe, sort of, kind of been following him since I'd met him in September when we had Career and Life Management class together. When I saw him sitting on the ledge, I instantly knew that he was upset. His wide shoulders moved up and down, his head was hanging down between his knees, hiding his dirty blond curls and the fat sideburns that stretched across his face. I squished myself down onto the ledge where he was sitting and put my arm around him. Izzy's a big guy, but he curled right into me like a kid.

I didn't ask what was wrong. It didn't matter. I just let him cry. My parka was soaked with his tears by the time he finally pulled himself upright. Wiping the tears from his face, he started to apologize. I put my hand on his cheek and shook my head, and then I leaned in to kiss him.

"This is a bad idea," he said when we came up for air. "The girl I want doesn't want me back, and I'm not in a good place, Davis."

I can't say he didn't warn me.

Still, from that January afternoon until yesterday, we were a couple. Sort of. It's not like he'd ever hold my hand in school or anything.

I walk down the wooden steps to get to the lookout point, lost in my best memories of Izzy. There are signs and fences to keep people out, so I always feel weird coming here. The path is super icy, and so many feet have compacted the snow that the improvised route looks almost permanent. Empty branches reach out, scratching my face, but still I press on.

I get to the ledge where Izzy and I sat that January day and so many days after that. He was always so sweet here, pulling me toward him in a way that he didn't do at school. Being with him, being around him, those were the first moments since the fire that I'd felt happy. That I'd felt totally safe.

Izzy would usually talk about his sister, Nakita, whom I already knew from all her YouTube videos about the tar sands. He'd talk about climate change and the pipeline project and the Climate Club he was determined to really get started, even though the first attempt by that Puerto Rican girl had fizzled. And I'd listen. I'm good at listening. Really good.

And when Izzy stopped talking, taking a breath, taking a break, I started. I told him about everything that happened after the fire. I talked about everything I'd done and how it had all blown up in my face. The look in his eyes — there was so much care there, so much admiration — it was almost like the way Porkchop used to look at me, only with less eye goop and better breath.

I hurl a snowball down to the frozen river. It doesn't even dent the ice. Maybe that's the way I can win Izzy back. I can change his mind about me if I somehow become the badass he thought I was all along.

RENZI

Renzi sees the duct tape before she sees the chocolate.

At the end of the hallway, from the top of her locker to its bottom, at least a dozen pieces of duct tape reflect the glare of the fluorescent lights overhead.

This is the Zángano's doing. She's sure of it.

Renzi groans as she approaches, far from happy that her instincts are correct. There's an expensive chocolate bar under each separate swatch of duct tape.

Fair trade, 90% cacao. Vegan. Wrapped in unbleached, compostable paper. No weird-sounding chemicals, no preservatives.

And in the middle of the locker, a bright red cardboard fist instead of a heart and the words "Be My Social Justice Valentine."

Renzi squeezes her eyes shut. It's too early in the morning to have to deal with this. Too early to recognize and accept that actions have consequences, even when those actions are seriously misinterpreted by the stupidest of stupid guys.

She doesn't even like this kind of chocolate.

Hates it, in fact. What's the point of eating super-ethical chocolate if it's so bitter that it makes your eyelids flutter in protest and your entire mouth collapse in on itself, cheeks sucked in so hard that your lips pucker up until you look like a fish?

Renzi pushes air out through her closed lips, the sound of a workhorse gearing up for an unpleasant chore. She has to get this off her locker before Jae sees it. Or that Davis girl.

But especially Jae.

Renzi can't believe she let Izzy kiss her last night. How could she have been so stupid? She glances at her phone: 8:47. Jae will be here any second.

Renzi tears down the fist with a single swipe, crumpling it and throwing it toward the recycling bin. (She misses, but it's close enough.) She rips the super-ethical chocolate bars down, two at a time. It would be too wasteful to throw them in the trash, but she doesn't want them anywhere near her, so she stomps down the hall and dumps them on a desk in the closest classroom. Happy Valentine's Day to whomever finds them.

When Renzi gets back to her locker, Jae's waiting. She's got a big smile on her face and her hand behind her back.

"Ta-dah!" Jae pulls a giant CaraMelt bar out from behind her, handing it to Renzi. It's sickly-sweet milk chocolate and cheap caramel, filled with orangutan-killing palm oil, synthetic emulsifiers and unpronounceable chemical preservatives. And it's wrapped in single-use plastic. It's all the things Renzi stands against. And it also happens to be her favourite food in the entire world.

"Your secret is safe with me," Jae whispers out the side of her mouth, her hand shielding her lips.

Renzi throws her arms around her best friend and holds her locked in a hug. And she keeps holding on. Jae doesn't hate anyone, but she sure loathes Izzy Malone. And there is no way Renzi will let the Zángano get between her and the best friend she's ever had.

DAVIS

I pull the lid off the Sharpie and take a step toward the wall closest to Izzy's locker. I'm launching my path toward Badassdom with graffiti, but I suddenly clue into the fact that Izzy probably won't recognize my handwriting. And it's not like I'm going to sign whatever I scribble on the wall. I take a step back. And then forward again. A few feet away, someone coughs. It's Ben.

He's wearing one of those #FortMacStrong T-shirts. It's weird to see it on him, partly because he usually wears geeky science shirts, but mostly because half the people who slammed me on Twitter included that hashtag after their comments. Ben asks me something, but I'm too distracted to register what he said.

"Cat got your tongue?" Ben asks as I shove the Sharpie in my pocket.

"What exactly do cats do with all these tongues they seize? Do they eat them? Are cats notorious for tongue eating? Or do they just store them up somewhere, in a giant stockpile of stolen tongues?"

Ben laughs. "Ah, Davis. The questions that keep you up at night."

It's not just the questions that stop me from sleeping. It's the stupid flashbacks. The bitch tweets. The meat envelope. But yeah, thinking about the international feline tongue-stealing conspiracy keeps me awake too.

I give Ben a little wave goodbye and rush around the corner to the girls' bathroom, looking left and right before I push the door open. No one is around to see me going in. All the stalls are empty too, so I have absolutely no excuses for inaction.

I inhale deeply, clench my teeth and lock the stall door behind me. I crouch down, my butt against my heels, and pull the lid from the Sharpie again. Or, at least, I try to. The lid won't budge. Maybe it's a sign that my planned graffiti is a bad idea, a doomed effort. I exhale, relieved, but then the lid slides right off, leaving me with no evidence of divine intervention and no more excuses. This graffiti will seriously anger a lot of people, just like my tweet did, but extreme times demand extreme actions. And even though Izzy isn't likely to enter the girls' washroom any time soon, I can text him a picture of it.

Our planet is on fire!
Our lives are in danger!
We need solar panels
NOT pipelines

Before I can add punctuation — a period or an exclamation mark or a dozen exclamation marks — someone walks into the bathroom. I freeze. Should I flush and run? Wait the other person out? I inhale, trying to determine if the Sharpie smells, if its scent will betray me.

I make my decision: flush and run. But just as the water whooshes in the toilet, I hear a string of angry swear words from the stall beside me.

At least, I figure they're curses because of the ferocity of the delivery. I don't know enough Spanish to be sure. There is only one girl in the entire school who shouts like this, only one person whose sharp questions in school assemblies and running commentaries about everything carry such force. And only one girl in the school who speaks this much Spanish. A quick glance below the stall wall dividing us confirms my guess: it's that grade-twelve girl Renzi Chan Cruz and her purple Converse sneakers.

I leave my stall, still thinking I might escape, but I can't do it. I have to see if she is okay or needs help. I knock gently on her stall door. "You okay in there?"

We aren't friends. But I've known about her since I saw her and Izzy talking during the first (and only) Climate Club meeting in September. Sure, if I had actually gone INTO the meeting, instead of just hovering outside the door, I probably would have impressed Izzy and maybe even become friends with Renzi. Too bad I can't get backsies on that day.

"Noooooooooo. I am definitely not okay. Hurricanes have trashed Puerto Rico, oil tycoons are destroying our planet, a new pipeline is coming and I'm sitting here wailing in the bathroom because of the stupidest of all problems." Renzi flings open the stall door and holds up outstretched palms — the universal signal for WHAT THE HELL AM I SUPPOSED TO DO NOW?

I have no idea what she means. When I shake my head in confusion, Renzi lets loose an exaggerated sigh and motions toward her bright blue pants. It takes me a couple of seconds, but then I see it: there's a nasty red stain blooming at her crotch. Oh.

"Wait right here," I say, jumping into action.

"As if I'd go anywhere."

I race to my locker, fighting to get the combination lock open as quickly as possible and — of course — missing the number thirty-seven. And then missing it again.

Breathe, Davis. Breathe. Twenty-eight . . . once past zero-six . . . directly back to thirty-seven.

Locker door finally open, I grab my emergency bag, slam my locker shut and run back to the bathroom.

"Okay," I say, struggling to catch my breath. "What do you want? Regular? Super? SuperPlus? Ultra-ultra? I only have the non-applicator kind because I think the applicators on regular tampons are totally wasteful, and I don't have any pads because, well, gross. I know I should use a period cup thing, but I don't because it doesn't really work for me, and oh my God that's way too much information. And I've got a spare pair of underwear and yoga pants too."

Inhale. Hold. Exhale. And again.

"Regular's good," Renzi says from inside her bathroom stall. I grab a couple of regular tampons from my bag, along with the emergency underwear and pants, and hand them to her under the door.

"You carry around extra clothes?" she asks.

"Trauma in grade-seven band class." No need to give details.

"*Gracias, amiga*," Renzi says when she exits her stall. She rolls her own pants into a tight cylinder and washes her slim, graceful hands. And then she wraps me in a tight hug. She makes the sound of a kiss as she presses her cheek against mine. "Your name's Davis, right?"

I have never been so happy to hear my name.

We head out of the bathroom, and just as she squeezes my arm to say goodbye, I realize just how badly I want to be friends with her. I've been following her online ever since my failed attempt to get over myself and join the Climate Club, and she always posts about Puerto Rico and the hurricanes. She went there over Christmas, visiting her grandparents four months after twin hurricanes downed power lines, tore roofs from homes, crushed roads like they were crackers and razed green forests. All those posts make me feel connected to her. After all, I know what it's like to lose everything when nature smacks back.

"Is your family okay? After the hurricanes, I mean?"

"Ay, *nena*," Renzi says, shaking her head. She pushes her spiral curls over her shoulder, the bottom two inches a bright shade of purple. "The hurricanes hit in September and my abuelos still don't have power. Still! I'm trying to get them a better generator but —" she breaks off suddenly, running away from me.

I watch, stunned, as she throws her body between some guy and the water bottle–vending machine.

"Our oceans are choking with plastic," she says, her finger

pointed at his face. "The water fountain is right there. Use it." And then she plucks the five-dollar bill right from his hand and tucks it in the pocket of his hoodie.

My mouth drops like a cartoon character. I have to hide in a bathroom stall, guaranteeing my anonymity before I speak out about environmental stuff, but Renzi just goes and acts directly. No hesitation. No fear. That was quite possibly the most amazing thing I've ever seen. The most un-Davis thing too.

"Screw off," the guy says, taking a threatening step toward her. He's not a small dude.

Renzi just tosses her hair over her shoulder and laughs. She skips back to me, lacing her arm through mine. "That was fun," she says. "Now, give me your number, *amiguita*."

Little friend.

And my brain is blown. Seriously. Blood splatter and grey matter all over the floor.

JAE

Jae opens the door that connects the garage to her house and dumps her heavy backpack on the floor. So much homework, so little time. She wanders into the kitchen, knowing that her mother won't be home until seven at the earliest, and she smiles at the sight of fresh vegan muffins on the counter. They're the super yummy and fluffy kind that only Jennylyn is capable of baking. Jae's mother has cut back Jennylyn's hours now that Jae is almost eighteen, and it sucks, even if it makes sense. Maybe Jennylyn could shift her schedule so that she's here when Jae gets home after school.

But Jae feels selfish for wanting that. Jennylyn has her own life. Her own kids.

Jae stuffs a muffin into her mouth and heads downstairs to check on the girls, Bertie, Broke Beak and Lala. Jae gently opens the door to their room, the small space under the stairs that Jennylyn kindly promised not to disturb, a tiny room Jae's mother probably has yet to even discover in their monstrosity of a house.

Lala's bustling about, cooing her afternoon greetings. Her foot looks better, healing faster than Bertie's wing is. The new warming light is on, generating just the right amount of heat.

"Howdy, sweeties," Jae says, stroking Bertie on the head. She spreads birdseed out for them and checks their water supply.

Jae had saved these birds, two injured pigeons and a sparrow that coos like a dove. She found Bertie in the park outside her house, trying to fly with a badly broken wing. Broke Beak had flown into a window at school, and Jae found Lala hobbling about downtown.

Rescuing these birds had been pretty straightforward. (And expensive too. But Jae had her mother's credit card to take care of the vet bills.) As soon as they are fully healed and able to fly again, she'll release them back into the wild. They were her first bird rescues. But as she strokes Broke Beak's head, Jae thinks again of all the birds she hasn't been able to help: horned larks found dead in Haus Oil's new oil sands mine in September, great blue herons killed because Haus hadn't stored its chemicals properly, and those sixteen hundred ducks that died nine years ago when they landed in the toxic puddle of Haus's oil sands leftovers. Even Jae's mom and her lawyerly bullshit hadn't been able to protect Haus from millions of dollars in fines.

Jae's phone warbles, the soft canary sound announcing a text.

Renzi: Want the good news or the bad first?
Jae: hello to you too.
Renzi: Haha

37

Renzi: With my paycheque tomorrow I'll finally have
   enough money for the solar generator
Renzi: !!!!!!
Jae: amazing! what's the bad news?
Renzi: . . . . . .
Jae: ?
Renzi: Izzy gave me half of it
Renzi: His Hardware Depot earnings
Jae: ewwwwww!
Renzi: I thought it was kind of sweet of him
Jae: ewwwwww!

If there is one guy Jae cannot stand, it's Izzy Malone.
He's so arrogant, so full of himself. The absolute worst part
is the way he constantly harasses Renzi, like he's trying to
wear her down even though she's rejected him a bunch of
times.

Jae's biggest regret is that she actually invited him to the
Christmas dance last year. It was just that for once in her
life, her mom had actually been excited about something
Jae-related. She bought Jae a fancy formal dress and made
a big deal about how Jae should find a cute boy to take as a
date, so Jae had chosen Izzy. Jae hadn't wanted to burst this
unexpected bubble of motherly affection. And that wasn't
Izzy's fault, it was Jae's. Still, when Izzy had kissed her at the
dance, it was easily the most disgusting thing imaginable. All
that slobber. All that hot minty toothpaste breath. All that
choking her with his tongue. Gross. So disgusting that this
was her first — and so far only — kiss. Gross, gross, gross.
That kiss was one of Jae's lowest moments ever, and every
time she sees Izzy, she cringes at the memory of it.

Jae: you know he's going out with that davis girl, right?
Jae: the death threat girl.

Jae has never actually met Davis Klein-Mah, but she's heard the rumours. Everyone has. Davis started at Strathearn High last May after escaping the Fort McMurray wildfire. She had tweeted something, blaming the fire on climate change and the Fort Mac tar sands, and somebody had called the school with some kind of threat. News like that travels fast, especially when a principal tells the teachers to keep it secret.

Jae feels a little sorry for Davis whenever she sees her in the hallways of the school. She always looks a little stunned, like a bird that has just flown into a window. But when Jae saw her walking on Whyte Avenue with Izzy's arm around her shoulder a month or so ago, Davis barely reaching up to his armpit and with a big, silly grin on her face, Jae's level of concern rocketed upward. That was not a relationship that was going to last long. And it definitely would not end well.

Renzi: I heard they broke up
Renzi: I thought I saw her writing graffiti by our lockers yesterday
Renzi: but then she just ran to the bathroom
Renzi: so I followed
Jae: weird.
Renzi: Totally weird
Renzi: Are we doing something this weekend?
Renzi: Like FINALLY hanging out at your place?
Jae: drowning in homework. sorry.

Jac doesn't like lying. And she especially doesn't like lying to her best friend. But Renzi has such passionate opinions about how McMansions destroy nature, about rich white women who exploit their Filipina nannies and about how the new Haus pipeline will make hurricane season so much worse, so lying is precisely what Jae will do.

DAVIS

I get off the train at Belgravia Station and walk in the light snow to the off-leash dog park. I made it through the whole post-dumping week at school without a major breakdown. And I only texted Izzy three times.

Fine. Three times a day. Every day except today. Because today I texted him four times. I pull out my phone to re-read what I sent.

> Davis: Do you want to go for a walk or something?
> Davis: Sometime, I mean. Not today. I know you
>   said you need space.
> Davis: There's a really good article on pipelines in Grist.
> Davis: I can send it to you if you want.

I am such a jackass. I can't believe I sent those. Four texts in just two hours this morning. And it's not like Izzy is responding. Why do I do this? It's like I get a little rush every time I click send and then crash immediately thereafter. I shove my phone into my back pocket and turn the corner to the dog park. I know it's super weird to go to the dog park without an actual dog, but I'm heading there all the same.

Q: What's the best way to stop sobbing about Izzy breaking my heart?

A: Distract myself with memories of the golden lab whose death broke my heart.

Healthy, I know.

I land a couple of blows on my legs, punching so hard my hand hurts, and then I pull off my mitten and start scratching that little patch on my head. I've been scratching this same spot for weeks — months, maybe — the same square inch on the left side of my head. My long brown hair has been worried down to just a prickly tuft in this one spot. It's probably an anxiety thing. I pull my hand off my head, shove it back into my mitten and push my hand deep into my parka's pocket. I need a human version of Porkchop's cone of shame, that giant plastic collar that kept her paws away from her wounds.

I've been standing here for maybe ten minutes when I feel a tap on my right shoulder. I turn, but no one's there. And on my left, Ben laughing. The Ben Cron special. I fall for it every time.

He hurls a chewed tennis ball over his shoulder, and a big white dog bounds after it, jumping through the snow.

"You didn't get a new dog, did you?" There's something in Ben's voice, an undertone of concern, that kind of makes my throat swell.

He must know that I haven't gotten a new dog.

If it were anyone else, I'd totally lie. Randomly point to a dog in the distance and claim it was mine. But I wouldn't lie to Ben. Especially about a dog.

I shake my head, carefully keeping my eyes trained straight ahead. I really, really don't want to break down in public. I throw a quick punch against my leg, my fat mitten cushioning the blow.

"Nah," I say quietly. "I just miss Porkchop."

Ben makes a sound as he nods. A soft kind of a grunt. He tugs his toque down lower over his freckly forehead, his sleepy blue eyes looking into mine. He pulls the slimy ball from his dog's mouth and scratches him behind the ears, then winds his arm back and hurls the ball into the air.

"My brother works in a camp up there. In Fort Mac. I don't think I ever told you that. He calls it a sausage factory. Nothing but dudes." Ben knows all about what happened to me, to my dog, so the rapid change of direction in our conversation makes total sense. No one else could ever follow the kinds of conversations Ben and I have.

"Does he like it there?" I ask. Fort Mac is the weirdest place in the world. It's got all these guys — young white guys with big trucks and way too much testosterone and way, way too much cash — but then it's also got this, like, amazing sense of community. The people who live there full time, who have families there, they all know each other and support each other. The people are super nice there, way nicer than here, in Edmonton, or where I lived before, in Calgary. And they're super diverse too. Our neighbours on one side were Nigerian, and on the other side, they were Mexican. And at least six girls in my class wore hijabs. I miss that. A lot.

Ben tosses the slimy tennis ball again, laughing as his dog leaps to try and catch it. "I don't know if he likes the city —

he mostly sticks to the work camp and then flies back here. He likes the money, though. He could've gone to university, but he became a rig pig instead."

I wince. You can't live in Fort McMurray and hear that expression without recoiling. I only lived there for two years, and even I can't stand the name.

And like he's read my mind, Ben says, "Tom hates it when I call him that. So, I totally call him that all the time. And he just laughs all the way to the bank."

"My cousin Carly's the same." It hurts to say her name. I really miss her. But that's one more relationship my tweet burned to a crisp. "She has a degree in environmental sciences. She came to Fort Mac for an internship and ended up staying after she fell in love with this guy from Newfoundland. They really love it there." And they totally hate me for having criticized it.

I have seen Carly only once since the fire. Mom and I were shopping at Southgate right after fleeing to Edmonton with literally only the clothes on our backs. We were moving like zombies as we chose shirts and pants off the rack. Mom slipped away to buy new shoes for work, and I headed to the dressing room just as Carly stepped out of a change room. She stood rock still when I hugged her, not even lifting her arms from her sides. I asked how she was doing, knowing she lost everything in the fire too, but she shook her head.

"Blaming the oil sands for Porkchop's death was not okay, Davis," Carly said. "That was like saying I was responsible for killing her because I work in the industry. You know how much I loved Porkchop. Talk about kicking me when I'm down."

Thinking about Carly makes my breath catch in my chest. I pull off my mitten on the hand that's furthest away from Ben and pinch my thigh as hard as I can, and then I do it again. And again, so hard that I almost yelp. I shoot a worried look at Ben, hoping that he hasn't seen the pinching.

"I gotta get going," I lie, coughing a bit so that Ben won't hear the catch in my throat. No more dog parks for me.

RENZI

Renzi pulls Jae's parrot-green sleeping bag up to her chin and then all the way over her head. Renzi hasn't returned the bag yet. With its warmth, the comfort it brings, the way it calms Renzi right down — the sleeping bag is like Jae morphed into camping gear.

Jae brought the sleeping bag over the night before the first of the hurricanes hit the Island in September. She'd walked through Renzi's unlocked front door, heading straight for the couch where Renzi, Lino and their mom sat curled up in terror, watching the swirling storm on their mom's laptop. Mami had called and called Abuela's cell phone and Abuela and Abuelo's neighbours and all their cousins, but no one answered. Renzi had never imagined silence could be so terrifying.

Jae had brought over containers of takeout food from the Cuban place, the closest thing you could get to Island food in Edmonton. And Jae had stayed. She'd slept on the floor of Renzi's room in her sleeping bag, refusing the bed. She'd done the laundry, vacuumed, gone for groceries, doing all the things that Renzi, Lino and Mami didn't have the strength to do. The hurricanes had knocked out power, internet and phone lines across the Island. Renzi, Lino and their mom didn't sleep for days, waiting for the phone to ring or a text to come through. Waiting for an email or a Facebook post — anything that would tell them if her grandparents and their extended family were okay.

Camilo texted to see if Renzi was okay, even though she'd broken up with him the month before because she'd needed space, some air and some room to figure out who she was without another boyfriend attached to her side. Izzy texted a lot too, angry messages blasting billionaires for the climate change that strengthened the storms. But only Jae had come to her house. Nobody else thought to do that.

Jae hadn't talked much, and she hadn't expected Renzi to talk either. She was just there, constantly, keeping Renzi together — keeping her, Lino and Mami going — until they finally got a phone call from the Island. A cousin of a neighbour's aunt was finally able to get cell service, finally able to pass on a message from Renzi's abuelos: they didn't have power, they didn't have running water, but they were okay. They were okay.

It had taken eleven days for that phone call to come. And Jae had stayed at Renzi's house, taking care of them that entire time. Mami had protested weakly, but Renzi could tell just how comforted she was by Jae's presence.

Jae's stay was the kindest thing anyone had ever done for Renzi. And now Renzi has gone and betrayed Jae by making out with the one guy who symbolizes something terrible

47

to Jae. Renzi had seen Izzy and Jae kissing at the Christmas dance back in grade eleven. She still remembers seeing Jae run from the gymnasium when that one slow song ended.

"Are you okay, nena?" Renzi had asked when she finally found Jae in the bathroom by their lockers, her eyes puffy and her face red. "Do I need to go and yell at Izzy Malone about consent?"

Jae shook her head and blew her nose. "No and no. I'm the one who started it. He's so gross. So, so gross. I'm totally not into him. At all, Renzi. It's just — my mom was so excited about —" Jae broke down here, leaving her sentence unfinished. When she stopped crying, she said, "I'm queer, Renzi. I don't know what I was thinking."

But Renzi knew. Sort of. There had to be a reason Jae was so secretive about her family. Her home. And she'd wait as long as necessary for Jae to figure it all out and to share her truths when she was ready. That's what both Mami and Lino had told her to do. Over and over again. Renzi pulled out her phone and requested an Uber to get Jae home.

And she tried her hardest not to feel hurt when Jae insisted on going home alone.

DAVIS

I rest my chin on my knees at the kitchen table, scrolling through photos from a newspaper story about Puerto Rico's hurricane damage. My left hand is on my head, scratching lightly on that same worry patch. I catch myself and shove my hand underneath my thigh to keep it away from my scalp.

I click on another photo and see miles of trees folded in half. Homes ripped open like dollhouses. Highways with holes that look like the footprints of angry giants. Images of the wreckage fly across my screen with each swipe of my finger.

Even though the photos look nothing like the ones I studied after the Fort Mac fire, frantically looking for shots of Porkchop in the hopes that she'd somehow survived, the pictures still send my mind rushing back to that horrible day last year.

May 3.

The day had started off pretty normal, even though the skies looked orange, and it already hurt to breathe the smoky air. I was at the dog park, the biggest one in Fort McMurray, and Porkchop was chasing mosquitoes when a woman screamed and started running. There, just a few feet from Porkchop, a little ball of black and white fluff was yapping and growling and snapping at a pit bull.

The pit bull did not look amused.

(With foot-long spools of drool hanging from its mouth, with its lips pulled back from its long, sharp teeth, the pit bull looked very pissed. And hungry.)

"Chompsky!" the woman yelled, "Come here!"

Before anything else could happen, Porkchop tilted her head and trotted over to the two dogs, gently put her mouth around the fluff ball and then carried the surprised little dog away by the scruff of its neck.

The pit bull barked, then its owner walked over and dragged him away by the collar.

Porkchop trotted right to the yelling woman and dropped the fluff ball at the woman's feet. I ran over too, incredibly proud of Porkchop.

The woman scooped Chompsky up and then smiled at me. "Thank you so much. I really owe you. My name is Laura, by the way."

In a blather of words, the woman started to explain that she was in Fort Mac writing a book about the tar sands. And with that single word — tar, instead of oil — Laura instantly revealed herself. Wherever she was from, she was an outsider, a snob. Most likely from Toronto. Or maybe Hollywood. Someone who looked down on all of us Fort Mac people, who thought that she knew better than we did, that all we needed was to be educated.

I tried the word out under my breath. Tar. It did fit with the handful of disturbing videos I'd seen on YouTube about the oil sands.

"I'm trying to get people in this province to wake up to the destruction caused by these tar sands. This is the biggest industrial project on the planet, and it's the worst thing for our climate. All this extreme heat, all of these horrible forest fires and droughts and floods, we can trace them back to the tar sands. This wildfire that's burning outside the city? You can thank the tar sands for it. I want my book to make people see that."

"I'm sure that will go well for you," I said under my breath. I couldn't tell if she heard me or not, but my words felt meaner than I had intended, so I smiled and wished her luck with her book. "Bye, Chompsky."

At 6:25 that same night, the entire population of Fort Mac was ordered to evacuate.

All ninety thousand of us.

Mom, Dad and I were having supper at Regal Pizza when the evacuation order came. Our waitress came to the table and told us the news, told us that the restaurant was closing and that we had to leave. "Don't worry about the bill, guys. Just be safe."

"Porkchop," Mom and I said at the exact same time.

We ran to our SUV and Dad pulled out of the parking lot before we even had our seatbelts on. Dad drove way too fast, scary fast, veering across lanes of traffic, accelerating through orange lights and taking corners so quickly that I thought our SUV might tip over.

But it was too late.

51

I saw the flashing police lights before I understood what they meant. Two police cars and three barricades, blocking access to the only road into and out of our neighbourhood. Maybe if we begged, the police would let us pass, even for just five minutes. Just long enough to get Porkchop.

Dad got out of the SUV before I could, and Mom followed. I opened my door too, but Mom turned and shook her head. "Stay here, Davis." Her voice cracked when she said it, emotion splitting her words. All I could do was obey.

I watched from the back seat as Mom and Dad pleaded with the police. I couldn't hear their words, but I could tell exactly what they were saying by the body language: crossed arms and shaking heads from the police; Mom falling into Dad as he closed his arms around her.

Mom and Dad were silent when they got back into the SUV. I reached my hand over Mom's seat to touch her shoulder. She squeezed my hand and then stifled a sob. None of us said anything.

Dad turned our SUV around, joining the convoy of thousands of cars and trucks and SUVs fleeing south to Edmonton. We had no clothes, no toothbrushes, no computers. And we did not have our dog.

I sat motionless as we drove, one vehicle in an endless line of vehicles. Out one window, I saw houses; out the other, tall trees in flames. And out the back, a billowing black cloud of smoke and ash. It was like something out of a movie. Only it wasn't a movie. It was my life.

The air in our car felt tight, oppressive. The smoke was so thick that Mom hit the recycle air button. There wasn't any fresh air to bring in. You could hear the fire outside, cracking

52

and crackling even louder than our engine. A newscaster spoke calmly on the radio, broadcasting instructions.

"Do you think there's a chance Porkchop made it out okay?"

She was locked inside our house. None of our neighbours had a key. I knew the answer to my question was no, but I wanted Mom and Dad to lie to me. To tell me that anything was possible. To say that the firefighters would save our home. To explain that the fire would spare our neighbourhood and that Porkchop would be fine.

"I don't know, sweetheart," Mom said. "I really don't know."

Two days later, we got our answer.

We were sitting in Auntie Sherry's Edmonton living room, on the long red couch that was pulling double duty as my bed. Mom's phone buzzed, and I knew, I just knew, that the news was bad. I pulled my legs up close to my body, wrapping my arms around myself. The smoke from the Fort Mac fire had made Edmonton's air thick and heavy, even though we were five hours to the south, but that smoke wasn't why I was finding it hard to breathe. I watched Mom's face as she checked her phone, and the cry that escaped from her mouth told me everything.

Our house was gone. All of our things were gone.

And Porkchop was gone.

JAE

Snow crunches under Jae's boots as she walks through Haven Ravine. The *chickadeedeedee* song of the tiny black and white birds fills her heart; the screechy cries of the blue jays are a needed antidote to their shocking beauty. Squirrels twitter, trying to frighten away the magpies, and every few minutes, she hears clumps of heavy snow falling off branches to the ground below.

But as comforting as the ravine's songs are, their melodies always remind Jae of the new noises her mother added to the park last year: bulldozers and chainsaws and forklifts, and truck after truck of building supplies needed to construct their new monster house. It was no surprise that her mother had found a legal loophole to allow for construction in this supposedly protected area.

No surprise at all.

"Maybe she just knows how much you love the ravine," Jennylyn had suggested one morning about a month after the construction started. "Maybe that's why she's building the house there."

Even now, over a year later, Jennylyn's suggestion stirs something inside Jae. The idea that Jae's mother knew her well enough, understood her well enough, that she'd make a grand effort to construct a home in a spot Jae adored — that is an amazing, beautiful thought. But there is no point in fantasizing. Dreaming only makes the truth hurt worse. And all Jae had needed to do to quash Jennylyn's theory was to raise her eyebrows and tilt her head.

Jennylyn had laughed as she resumed mopping. "But probably not."

No. The only reason Jae's mother had torn through the ravine's dense green expanse, destroying birds' nests and feeding areas in the process, was because she wanted to prove she could.

"The house we have is good enough, Mom. Don't build something that's going to trash the ravine," Jae had pleaded with her mother.

"Jae, if I had wanted to settle for 'good enough,' I'd still be on the farm in Saskatchewan. If your grandparents had settled for 'good enough,' I'd have been born in East Germany. We don't settle in this family. You'd do well to learn that."

There was more to her mother's comment, Jae knew. An unspoken criticism that Jae was good, but not good enough. Good grades, but not good enough. Good at skiing and dancing and whatever other extracurriculars Jennylyn chauffeured her to, but not good enough. Never quite good enough.

Her mother would no doubt be polite and formal if Jae ever brought Renzi to the house — if her mother happened to be home from the office — but it would be way too embarrassing to show Renzi her three-million-dollar monster house when Renzi, her brother and mom live in a small townhouse that was probably built in the 1960s. And this particular three-million-dollar monster house is all the more mortifying given that it's smack in the middle of ravine land that everyone had assumed was protected from development. How could Jae show Renzi her house when Renzi was probably one of the thousands of people who'd signed the petition against the home's construction?

Or maybe Jae just doesn't want to out herself as a spoiled rich girl.

Jae squeezes her eyes shut, forcing thoughts of her mother from her head. She passes a tall white spruce tree and a blue jay dives right in front of her, squawking. Two tiny chickadees fly away, frightened by the beautiful but aggressive bully. That blue jay immediately reminds her of Izzy Malone in the cafeteria today. He'd waltzed over to Jae and Renzi's lunch table, with the confident stride of the hottest hot shit. He'd grabbed an empty chair and spun it around, throwing one of his long legs over it. He was wearing that hot pink shirt of his, the one with THIS IS WHAT A FEMINIST LOOKS LIKE written across the front in huge white letters. Jae's eyes rolled so far back in her head, there was a chance she'd never see again, and she got the hell out of the cafeteria before she had to spend even one second longer in his presence.

But Izzy can't be that bad, can he? All the girls at school seem to adore him. Even Renzi. And he did help Renzi buy that solar generator for her grandparents in Puerto Rico. Jae had helped too, but not as much as Izzy did. And Izzy isn't rich like Jae. Jae knows it's not Izzy's fault that she was trying to please her mother by inviting a guy to the Christmas dance. But still, the thought that she'd actually let Izzy put his tongue in her mouth makes Jae want to gag, to spew owl pellets of undigested bones, fur, claws and teeth all over the place.

If Izzy dares go over to the Wild Earth Animal Rescue, where that Kat girl works, Jae will seriously lose her shit. That would be the absolute and total last straw.

Oh.

Right.

Duh.

Jae groans. And then she laughs, a full-on belly laugh that rocks through her. She gets it now. She finally, finally gets it. She understands why he drives her bonkers. Izzy is a conceited ass, for sure, and she should never, ever have let him kiss her at the dance. But there's an edge of envy that taints her feelings about him. He's so confident in himself, so sure that he'll get whatever he wants and so certain he'll get everyone's attention and adoration — that's why Jae can't stand him. Because of that certainty, that surety; Izzy has it, and Jae definitely does not.

Maybe it's time to tell Renzi the whole truth. About her mother, her oil money, Jennylyn and the McMansion. Just to put it out there, get it said. Jae always thought she'd tell Renzi the truth about her mother if and when Renzi asked, but she never wanted to raise the issue herself. Unlike Izzy Malone, Jae has never liked being the centre of attention or the topic of discussion. But it's time. It's definitely time.

DAVIS

"Is that a new suit? It looks really nice."

Mom is in the kitchen, packing herself a lunch and — I think — a supper too. I guess she needs to stay late at the office. Again.

She nods and moves her lips upward in the motions of a smile. She looks exhausted and way too skinny, but it would be way too hurtful to say that to her.

"Thanks, sweetheart. One of the mechanical engineers dragged me to the mall yesterday. It's nice to have something that actually fits. I guess."

Mom lost twenty pounds over the summer, even though she definitely did not need to lose weight, so none of the clothes she bought right after the fire fit anymore. I overheard her tell my Auntie Lisa that she lost all that weight because she was so worried about me and kept forgetting to eat. I wonder if my aunt told Carly that, giving my cousin another reason to continue ghosting me.

I pull my phone from my pocket and send yet another set

of messages to my cousin, texting into the ether.

> Davis: Hi Carly! I saw you in that new ad about reclamation projects.
> Davis: I know you're doing really good work.
> Davis: Turning the mined areas back into wetlands and stuff.
> Davis: I'm really sorry if my tweet hurt you or offended you.
> Davis: Anyways, I miss you. Hope you're good.

I scroll up through months of unanswered texts, unanswered apologies. You know, just for the fun of making myself feel even worse about everything.

Mom steps toward me and gently lifts my hand from my head. I hadn't even realized I was scratching again. "Want me to make you another appointment with Jolene?" Mom asks.

Oh, God. No. Please. Jolene is this therapist Mom and Dad made me see this summer. For five straight sessions, she talked at me about cyberbullying and "making smart choices" about what I shared on social media. She wore so much perfume that my eyes streamed water, which she probably mistook for tears. And so many perfume molecules got stuck to my clothes and hair that Mom had allergy attacks when she picked me up after appointments. Mom and Dad finally let me stop seeing her when I promised to permanently delete Twitter from my phone. From my life.

But it's not like I can unsee the bitch tweets.

Or unsmell the burned piece of meat taped to my locker.

I give Mom a tight hug, trying to squeeze her into believing that I am fine. "I'm sorry you have to go into work on a Saturday," I say, but she just shrugs. She's been working most weekends lately. As soon as she's out the door and off to work, I move through the house, shutting off lights, lowering the thermostat and unplugging appliances that suck power even when not in use. After I shut off the last light, I feel wound up and unsatisfied, like I'm only getting started. This isn't enough.

Not anywhere close to enough.

Anything that I do on my own will be overshadowed one thousand billion times over by the oil company my parents work for. And not only do they work for Haus, they're actually engineers on the exact pipeline project Izzy is so upset about. That I'm so upset about. Things would be a lot easier if I disliked my mom and dad. If I could just be a normal teenager in angsty rebellion against her parents.

No such luck.

I head to the bathroom, my preferred spot for existential crises. I need the tininess of the enclosed spot, the tightness of the space between bathtub and toilet, without the darkness or fabric softener smells of a closet. I know I have to speak out against the pipeline, do something about it. That's the only possible thing that will win Izzy back. But I can't. I just can't.

You try having an entire province hate you. See what that does for your courage.

I lean in toward the bathroom mirror, taking a long, hard look at myself. My face is buried somewhere underneath the layers of foundation and contour and eyebrow pencil and eyeliner and mascara. Ella and Emma spent all of July and August giving me makeup tips and dragging me to the mall to buy some new concealer or contour or bronzer or whatever. I was so out of it, so stunned by all that had just happened, that I just followed along and did what they said. And it was like the more time I spent with them, the more layers I added to my face.

One look at Renzi, and anyone can tell she's a badass. The bright purple curls, the funky clothes in clashing rainbow colours, the septum ring.

Especially the septum ring.

I turn on the cold water, grab the soap and start excavating my face. I wash and wash until my skin feels raw. When all the makeup is gone, I stare at my naked face. I look younger without all the makeup. But older too.

Time to go and get my nose pierced.

RENZI

Renzi plucks the septum ring from her nose. A quick downward tug: no pain, no blood, because her septum isn't actually
pierced. She got the fake ring on the Island over Christmas,
and she likes how it keeps a physical reminder of Puerto
Rico in her line of sight at all times. Lino teases her about
it relentlessly, just like he ribs her about how much Spanish
she's been dropping into her speech ever since the hurricanes
hit the Island.

"You're trying too hard, Renzita," he said just that morning. "I think everyone already knows you're Puerto Rican.
You can stop reminding them every five minutes."

Sometimes she really hates her older brother.

Renzi pops the septum ring back in. Like so much else
about her — her bravado, her purple curls, her unflagging
confidence — the septum ring is something most people
think is 100% real. But Jae knows the truth. Jae knows
everything, always.

From grade seven until she broke up with Camilo this

past August, Renzi went through boyfriend after boyfriend after boyfriend. Boys were so much simpler than girls: none of the drama, none of the complications, none of the soul-wrenching, backstabbing, vomit-inducing manipulations suited only for the world of *telenovelas*. Things are just easier with boys.

"It's because of *Papi*, you know," Lino declared at dinner one night, pointing his fork at Renzi across the table. "You're afraid of the intimacy of friendship because Dad left. And so you just race through all these guys, tossing them aside the second you actually start to like them."

Renzi threw a *tostón* at him. She wished she'd thrown a knife.

"*Basta*, you two. Enough!" Their mother had swatted Renzi's hand gently, a wry smile on her face. "As long as Renzita is being responsible, her love life is none of our business."

Renzi didn't know if Lino was right or not. All she knew was that girls were a pain. None of them liked her, anyway. She knew what they said about her: that she was arrogant, conceited, that she thought she was better than them. So she just stuck with boys.

Then she met someone different.

Strathearn's a huge school, so Renzi had never even noticed this girl until their hands landed on the same Naomi Klein book in the Strathearn school library on the second day of grade eleven. Naomi Klein was Renzi's favourite Canadian activist. Actually, Naomi Klein was Renzi's favourite Canadian, period. And Renzi needed, absolutely needed, to have the new book in her possession. She had already planned the photos she would post of herself reading the book, eyes peeking out over the top. Now, if Renzi had been generous, she would have let the other person take it. But Renzi was not generous. She wanted that book. And she wanted it even more now that there was competition for it. So she curled her fingers around the book, locking her knees into place and narrowing her eyes in a challenge.

"Did you seriously just growl at me?" the girl asked, an amused look on her face. The girl tightened her own grip on the book and pulled it toward her. Renzi yanked it back, tearing it from the other girl's hands with such force that the girl stumbled a bit.

The girl's mouth dropped, in shock or surprise. She adjusted her horn-rimmed glasses and flipped her long brown hair over her shoulder. And then she hooted. A laugh like an explosion, loud and sharp. The laugh was not what Renzi had been expecting. Not at all. And the shock of it, the joy of it, made Renzi laugh too. She couldn't help it.

And then the girl grabbed the book back and ran.

"Come on," the girl called to Renzi over her shoulder. "We have a book to read."

Renzi and Jae have been inseparable for the year and a half since. Renzi's first close female friend.

Her only one, really.

DAVIS

"This really isn't how you're supposed to do it," Pink-Haired Barbie warns, positioning the earring gun over my nostril. "This is how we pierce ears, not noses. This isn't even the right kind of stud."

All the piercing places in Edmonton require parental consent for those under eighteen. (Even the six-hundred-dollar All-You-Can-Stand Tattoo place asks for ID.) I briefly considered my German great-grandma's method: frozen potato, needle and a lightning-fast hand.

I ended up going to the mall instead.

"Are you sure you want to do it this way?"

I nod. Pink-Haired Barbie shrugs and then pulls the trigger. I flinch, startled by the punch of pain.

"Hope you're prepared," Barbie says, tapping the counter with her sparkly purple fingernails as I pay.

"For infections?"

"For booger jokes."

Those jokes definitely will not come from Emma and Ella.

Nope. In my circles, the only one likely to honk out a big, sticky joke about snot is me. And possibly Ben.

"Are you picking your nose?" Ella asked Emma by our lockers the other day when Emma was obviously just scratching her nostril.

"Nah," I said. "Emma likes the one she was born with." And then I laughed at my own joke. Loudly.

Emma and Ella grimaced, but at least Ben leaned over and said, "Snot that funny, Davis."

I adore that guy.

Anyway, I know my nose ring will get Izzy's attention. I know it will surprise him. And at this point, with my dozens of texts to him left unanswered, any attention from Izzy will be good attention.

The massive stud in my nose twinkles in the fluorescent light of the train. My nostril is throbbing, and I can tell that every last passenger is either staring at my nose or desperately trying to avoid staring.

My phone buzzes against my thigh and my heart leaps right up into my throat. Maybe it's Izzy, finally responding to my texts. Wanting me back. Yes, yes, yes and yes.

It is not Izzy.

It's Mom.

"Don't be mad," I rush to say. The call will only last a few seconds, before the train flies back into the tunnel. I don't know why I texted her my picture.

Wait. Yes, I do — because I didn't want to get in trouble.

"I'm not mad, Davis. It looks cute. You're sixteen and it's your body after — " The tunnel cuts my mother off.

Cute?

Come on.

Cute is not the impression I'm going for.

Cute won't win Izzy back. Only finding some way to speak out against the pipeline and the tar sands will. I can't nose pierce my way back into his heart.

My phone buzzes again.

And this time, it will be Izzy. I know it.

Renzi: Store is dead, come visit
Renzi: Red Caboose Consignment 80604 104 St

As far as second bests go, this is as good as it gets.

An old-fashioned bell tinkles above the door as I walk in, stomping my feet to get the heavy snow off my boots. It's really, really hard to make Albertans take climate change seriously when winter usually lasts until June. That's why I've stopped calling it global warming or even global heating. In this deep-freeze province, the prospect of warming sounds really, really amazing.

Renzi jumps at the sound and then grins. "Davis! Thank God! I'm dying here."

She taps her phone and holds it out for me to see. It's a Twitter account. Just seeing that little blue bird at the top of the white screen sends my heart racing. And not in a good kind of way. My hand lifts to my head, but I catch it quickly and shove it in my pocket.

"GreenAída? Who's that? Sounds like a country." I laugh at my own joke about the Twitter handle, but Renzi narrows her eyes and tilts her head. Frack.

Way to go, Davis. A joke about Spanish. I hate it when people make jokes about how Mandarin and Cantonese sound, but there I go and make a joke about Spanish. Way. To. Go.

"She's me," Renzi finally says. "If you're already on Twitter, you need to start following me. If you're not, then get on and start following me." She looks again at her screen and then at me. "I definitely like your no-makeup look." Her silence about my nose stud registers with a thud. There's no way that she hasn't noticed it; my throbbing nostril is glowing redder than Rudolph's.

"GreenAída," I try again, needing to fix this. I really want Renzi to like me. "That's rad." But it isn't. Not really. Not at all, actually. It sounds like a cheap, sugary drink. Or a reusable bandage.

The bell above the door tinkles again, rescuing me from whatever additional stupidities were about to pour out of my mouth.

"Jae!" Renzi hollers, running over to the girl who has just come into the shop. I recognize her immediately: Renzi's girlfriend. Or at least I think she is. They're together constantly, laughing and yelling in their corner of the cafeteria while I sit with Ben (on a good day) or Emma and Ella (on a bad one). Renzi and Jae are always arm in arm, or Renzi is resting her feet on Jae's thighs.

Renzi throws her arms around Jae and plants a fat kiss on her cheek. "You came!"

"Course. Couldn't let my favourite *Boricua* spend her Saturday alone. We Islanders have to stick together." She nods at me in greeting, sets two huge bags of clothes on the counter and then hoists herself up beside them. She takes off her horn-rimmed glasses and starts to dry them on her bell-bottom jeans. I am officially buried under an avalanche of cool.

"I'm Jae."

"Davis."

Jae holds out her fist for a bump, waving her fingers in the air when our hands separate.

"Are you Puerto Rican too?" The number of Canadian Puerto Ricans I've met is increasing at an exponential rate.

"She wishes!" Renzi hoots, leaning on the counter beside Jae.

"I'm just a white girl," Jae says as she shakes her head, grinning. "But I was born on Vancouver Island, so I'm an Islander by default."

Renzi tears into the bags, pulling out dresses and blouses and purses and pants. Every third item still has a tag attached. "There's thousands of dollars of stuff in here, Jae. Are you *sure* your mom is okay with you selling this stuff?"

Jae swings her legs onto the counter and kicks one of the bags. "Don't worry, it'll take at least twenty-eight more loads before she'll even notice something's missing. More, probably."

Jae pulls a sparkly green scarf from the bag and hands it to me. "This would look really beautiful on you, Davis. And now," Jae turns to Renzi, "can you puh-lease turn off this noise and put on some *actual* music?" She grabs Renzi's phone and starts strumming her finger across the screen. "I cannot begin to understand how you can love poetry and still insist that *reggaetón* is music." Jae taps Renzi's phone dramatically and a throbbing pulse of drums and synthesizers bursts into the consignment store. She jumps off the counter right as Renzi lunges for the phone and starts gyrating to the thumping sounds of techno, all while Renzi jumps to try and grab her phone back.

The Renzi and Jae Show. I could watch it for hours.

When Jae finally relents and returns the phone, Renzi lightly taps Jae's butt.

"How long have you guys been together?" Ages, I'd guess.

Jae and Renzi look at each other, frowning, and then Renzi catches my eye and gives her head an almost imperceptible shake. Jae breaks the weirdly protracted silence with a warm laugh and then throws her arm around Renzi's shoulder. "Sure, I'm queer, but do you really think I could go out with someone who likes reggaetón?" She shudders.

"We're just friends, Davis," Renzi says, squeezing Jae's hand. "We're like Amy Poehler and Tina Fey. She's Tina, I'm Amy. I'm Shang-Chi and she's Katy Chen. Or whatever Puerto Rican-Chinese–white girl superfriend combo exists."

"You're part Chinese? You don't loo—" The words tumble out of my mouth before my brain has the chance to stop them. What is the ONE thing I hate hearing about my appearance? That I look Chinese or I don't look Chinese. That I must look only like my Mom. Or that I must look only like my Dad. As though it's anyone's business. And here I am, saying the same thing. Out loud, no less.

I need to fix this. Fast.

"Wow. I seriously can't believe I said that. I HATE it when people tell me that I don't look Chinese, and they say it all the time. The only other thing I hear as often is that I really,

really, really look Chinese. And —"

Jae puts her hand on my shoulder. Rescuing me. "We all say stupid stuff sometimes. Well," she says, "at least Renzi does."

"Seriously, though. I'm always saying the wrong thing." I wrap the green scarf around my hands and pull it so tightly that it hurts. "The shhhushers — these girls, Emma and Ella, in my grade — are forever groaning at my jokes or telling me to lower my voice, but —"

"They shush you?" Renzi interrupts. "That's horrible!"

Jae clears her throat and motions for me to keep talking. It's all the invitation I need to share the stuff that's battering around in my brain.

"Words and I don't get along these days. My boyfriend — ex-boyfriend — Izzy Malone seemed to like the stuff I have to say about climate change and the tar sands, but now he's dumped me because I didn't say enough. And Ella and Emma think I say too much. So maybe the reason Izzy dumped me isn't even about what I said or didn't say. I honestly don't know. Maybe I'm not hot enough. Or maybe he likes someone else."

I shake my head, blow air out of my mouth so forcefully that my lips flutter. "I'm pretty sure it's because he thought I'd be more outspoken about this new pipeline and stuff. I didn't speak out about it in front of his dad when I should have, and I let Izzy down."

Jae gently pulls the scarf from my hands. "Interesting. Izzy Malone is a goober, but I bet the reason he broke up with you has nothing at all to do with you. Renzi?" She looks at Renzi over her glasses. "Do you have thoughts on the matter?"

Renzi looks up and points her finger at Jae. "Shhhhhhhh."

JAE

Holding a grudge against unicorns is easier than you might expect.

A lot easier, actually.

Jae's hostility toward the mythical creatures dates all the way back to grade five when Mr. Shipley asked the class to name as many extinct animals as possible. He chuckled when Jae suggested unicorns.

"Oh," she'd said, her face burning with embarrassment. "You mean they're only endangered?"

To this day, Jae maintains that her question had not deserved the torrents of laughter it triggered. Narwhals exist — little whales with beautiful, helix tusks spiralling out of their heads. Horned screamers exist — Amazonian birds with long spiny horns that stretch up from their crowns. And, really, are rhinos so different from unicorns?

Her anti-unicorn grudge only grew over the years. For Jae's tenth birthday, her mother's assistant bought her a toy unicorn that pooped glitter slime. The gift was better suited for a child half Jae's age, with about one-eighth the brain power. If only her mother had tasked Jennylyn with buying a gift, things would have been fine. Just thinking about that glitter-pooping toy — or about unicorns in general — makes Jae grind her teeth together. Jae doesn't like reacting this way; rage against make-believe animals is not in keeping with good mindfulness practice.

But unicorns now stand a chance at redemption. A couple of days ago, Premier Nancy Reese bounced onto the stage at a press conference, her sleek, silvery hair shining under the spotlights. She was announcing her government's plan to get Haus's Trans-Provincial Pipeline built, no matter the opposition coming from environmental groups or politicians in neighbouring British Columbia. When a journalist in the crowd asked a question about transitioning away from fossil fuels because of the climate change emergency, about using all of those millions of government dollars to subsidize solar and wind projects instead of a new oil pipeline, Premier Nancy scoffed. "These fantasies are nice," she asserted, "but they're not realistic. Fantasies won't fund our province, fantasies won't put food on the table of actual working families. In this province, we ride horses, not unicorns."

We ride horses, not unicorns. The premier's comment immediately became a meme, repeated over and over by the pipeline's supporters — as if those panicking about climate change are the ones living in a ridiculous fantasy when they are actually the ones with their eyes open to scientific realities.

Premier Nancy's comment is almost enough to make Jae reconsider her long-standing hostility toward unicorns. Jae even considered adding the hashtag #Unicornrider to her social media posts. And she'd been thinking about unicorns when she walked by the Wild Earth Animal Rescue yesterday and looked in the window. Just casually. Just in case Kat was working.

She was. And she waved and smiled at Jae.

Next time, Jae will go inside. Talk to her. Learn more about her. Get to know her. Be around her. Jae grinned all the way home.

The giddy, light feeling that seeing Kat generated feels so honest and so real that Jae feels inspired to start sharing her truths with Renzi this morning.

Jae fidgets beside Renzi's locker, shifting from one foot to the other as her friend removes her coat and mittens. She's not totally ready to tell Renzi about her McMansion or her mother, but she can start by telling Renzi about Jennylyn, the person who is more of a mom to Jae than anyone. She knows Renzi will take the news in stride, even though Renzi often accuses nameless rich white women of exploiting Filipina nannies. Renzi has schooled Jae in the historical connections between Puerto Rico and the Philippines — their parallel experiences of colonialism and plunder and resistance — but Renzi will for sure see how much Jae adores Jennylyn. Jae will even ask Renzi if she wants to meet Jennylyn, maybe at a coffee shop or a park. Jae knows she is making way too big a deal out of something she doesn't want to cast as a HUGE REVEAL, but she is nervous all the same — an energetic, happy kind of nervous, but still nervous.

"Are you okay, amiguita? You're acting weird."

Here we go. The time has come. It's time to share her

first truth with Renzi. The Jennylyn truth. Jae takes a deep breath and closes her eyes.

And then Renzi laughs. A big, explosive, roaring laugh.

From out of nowhere, Izzy is suddenly here. He's on his hands and knees in front of Renzi, trying to buck his feet in the air. And failing miserably. He keeps toppling over and then trying again. That guy is nothing if not persistent. He is dressed in tight white pants and a white turtleneck, a glittery silver tail cascading from his rear and a plush unicorn hat, complete with horn and mane, covering his head. He has an old-fashioned camera — one of those that spits out instant pictures — hanging on a strap around his neck.

"In this province," he shouts, "we ride UNICORNS!" He bucks his legs into the air a couple more times, which Renzi seems to find utterly hilarious, and then he rears up into a standing position and pulls the camera over his head. He thrusts the camera into Jae's hands, gets down on his hands and knees again, and pats his back. Jae can practically hear Izzy's next line. Something crude about saving a horse by riding a unicorn.

"Hop on, ladies. One at a time, please. Renzi, you first. I'm going to flood the premier's office with these. Picture postcards of people who care about the environment, riding a unicorn. I've taken pictures with everyone in the hallway and now it's your turn."

"Take the picture, Jae!" Renzi says, laughing as she sits down on Izzy's back. "Then I'll take one of you!"

"I'm late for class," Jae says flatly, even though there's still plenty of time. She puts the camera on the floor in front of Izzy's face — not dropping the camera, but not being especially gentle either — and rushes away. Renzi calls out after her, but Jae keeps walking.

"Jae!" Renzi catches up with her, grabs her arm. "What the hell? I know you don't like Izzy, but, come on — that was a good idea. It was funny. And it's for a good cause. It's just a postcard. He's taking pictures with everyone, not just me. Don't be like this."

"Like what?" Jae feels the icy bitterness dripping from her question. She feels so hurt. So frustrated. She was finally about to be honest with Renzi, and that got interrupted by the very guy who embodies Jae's dishonesty with herself. The very guy she'd let kiss her because of some stupid need to get her mom's approval.

Renzi just crosses her arms and shakes her head, her purple curls bouncing.

It's too much for Jae. It's all too much.

"Forget it, Renzi. Don't answer that. I'm just working through a lot of things, okay? And Izzy Malone has an amazing ability to block me from doing that."

Jae turns to leave, but Renzi reaches out, touches her shoulder. "You know you can tell me anything, nena," Renzi says, a hurt look on her face. Jae nods and rushes away, not trusting herself to keep it together.

"Upstaged by a fucking unicorn," Jae says as she turns the corner. She says it so loudly that those blond girls Davis hangs out with — the ones who always dress the same and walk the same and talk in the same hushed tones — turn from their lockers and shoot Jae matching baffled looks.

The way those girls look at her, the way they are so fully and totally confused by her, hits Jae like a punch. Renzi would never react to Jae that way. Ever. Guilt rushes into the void left by anger. She shouldn't have snapped at Renzi like that. She definitely shouldn't have shut Renzi out like that. It was selfish. Cowardly. Jae needs to be more like a unicorn: stop horsing around with her truths and get to the freaking point.

DAVIS

"What the what?" Ella's rapid-fire words are laced with giggles. "And then I put the eyelash on backwards, and it looked so janky in the upper corner that I just pulled it off and started again. But oh my gosh, it felt like I was peeling my eye right off!"

It's exhausting just trying to follow her words. I can almost see the exclamation marks flying out of her mouth.

"You know that eyelash glue is made of formaldehyde, right?"

"I'm wearing the magnetic ones," Emma chimes in, ignoring me. "My eyelids feel soooooo heavy, but I love them."

"Oh no!" I lift my metal water bottle into the air, levitating it toward Emma's face. "The magnetic force is too strong . . . the pull . . . the pull."

"Volume, Davis," Ella says. "Shhh."

Enough. I can't do this anymore. I can't pretend we're friends.

"Um, oh, I forgot. I have to talk to that girl Renzi about,

um, getting a job where she works. Gotta run." I shove all my food back into my lunch box — an old Muppet Show metal one that I'd found at Value Village — and rush to the other side of the lunchroom. I tap Ben lightly on the shoulder as I walk past, trying to slow myself down and look natural as I hurry toward Renzi and Jae.

"Can I sit with you guys?"

I pinch my leg, waiting for the answer.

"Caramba, nena! Sit already! That's your problem: you always think you have to ask permission. Stop. Just stop. And do it." Renzi drags a chair out from the table and yanks on my arm, pulling me down.

Jae scoots her chair over and then points to the unsliced cucumber, muffin and apple that I set out on the lunch table. "You're vegan?"

"How do you know someone's vegan?" Renzi asks before I can answer Jae's question. She delivers the question in a way that I can tell a punchline is coming.

"Don't worry. They'll tell you." Renzi guffaws at her own joke; Jae rolls her eyes and shakes her head. As she does, one of her earrings flies out and lands by my elbow. It's a tiny silver hummingbird. As I hand it back, Jae says, "I'm kind of a bird geek."

"Kind of, amiguita?"

"That's a cheeeeeep shot," I pause, waiting to land my line. "And hard to swallow."

Jae doesn't laugh. Renzi doesn't laugh. They just look at each other, and then back at me. Maybe they don't know that a swallow is a kind of bird. Or that I meant cheep like a bird, not cheap like stingy. Or maybe my joke was way too dorky. Too corny. Too spectacularly bad. No wonder Emma and Ella always shush me.

Jae threads her earring back in and glares at me. "I've heard those jokes before. You're just parroting others."

I am about to apologize when Jae's pun registers in my brain. And for once, I have a snappy comeback. "Owl not give up."

"Toucan play at that game, my friend."

We both explode with laughter. Jae laughs so hard she snorts, which makes me laugh even harder. So hard it hurts, but in a good kind of way. It's the kind of laughter I haven't experienced in ages. Maybe even since fleeing Fort Mac.

"Oh my God, you guys are such nerds!" Renzi shouts, feigning horror. "I am officially surrounded by bird nerds. BIRD NERDS!" She shudders.

"The proper term, Renzi, my friend," Jae says, looking serious, "is bird brains." And that sets us off again.

Whenever I roll out puns with Emma and Ella, they respond with strained smiles. "Cute," Ella always says. "Sure," Emma always adds.

But Renzi and Jae hoot so loudly my ears hurt. And that is when I know for sure: I have found my people.

Finally.

JAE

Sorry, sorry and sorry.

"Oh, Jae," she scolded herself. She knew her behaviour in the hallway with Izzy the Moronic Unicorn was very sorry indeed. Jae has already apologized to Renzi, but she still feels rotten about the lousy way she acted. She knows Izzy didn't technically do anything wrong, and so, here she is now, standing on Whyte Avenue in the snow, trying to make things right. She tapes a homemade poster to a lamp post — a cute cowgirl riding a unicorn, with the words What's More Imaginary Than a Unicorn? "Ethical" Oil. STOP THE HAUS PIPELINE!

Jae works her way down the street, taping and shivering, shivering and taping.

She only has a few posters left when she feels a hand on her shoulder. Before she even turns to see whose hand it is, the pulse of lightning that shoots through her parka from her shoulder to her toes tells her it is someone good.

The lightning does not lie.

Kat is there, making Jae's heart skip with her wry smile and spiky brown hair.

"Can I have a sign?"

Jae blinks at Kat's question. A sign to show Kat how much she likes her? A sign to show how much she cares?

Not breaking eye contact with Jae, Kat reaches down and takes a flyer from Jae's hand.

Oh. That kind of sign.

Jae holds onto the flyer that Kat took. Jae knows enough about physics to understand that paper does not conduct electricity, at least not under normal circumstances. But Kat clearly defies the natural laws of the universe because the piece of paper connecting her to Jae practically sparks with energy and tension.

Kat's eyes widen as she looks at the flyer, and Jae feels a pulse of panic. Most people in this province, even if they care about the environment and worry about climate change, want the pipeline. They still think it's the best thing for the province, for the economy and — some of them — even for the environment. What if Kat is one of those people? What if Kat rejects her over this?

"Interesting," Kat says. Her eyebrow is raised, but she is still smiling. "You know that moving oil by pipeline is way safer, way better for animals than moving it by train, right?"

Jae nods. Kat's right about the risks of trains, but the pipeline isn't the real problem. It's the way a pipeline would expand the tar sands, because more tar sands would mean more harm to so many more birds. All those birds. But, for the first time in as long as she can remember, Jae doesn't want to talk about birds.

"I do know that," she says with a shy smile, "and I know why the pipeline's still terrible. But if you let me buy you a hot chocolate, I promise I won't say a single thing about why I'm right and you're wrong. I, Jae, will not make a peep about it."

Kat threads her arm through Jae's. "Deal. I'll keep my opinions to myself too. Like the cat has my tongue."

Jae tries very, very hard to stop from grinning. She does not succeed.

DAVIS

I find Renzi's latest GreenAída tweets by doing an internet search on her Twitter handle. There's no way I'm actually rejoining Twitter. Not after what happened. I punch my right thigh repeatedly as I scroll through the tweets that Google shows me. Renzi has been posting a ton about the new pipeline and how it's going to make climate change so much worse by increasing production in the tar sands. Is the same thing going to happen to her that happened to me?

Memories of my wretched Twitter disaster pile into my mind, and I can't keep them out.

I was standing in Auntie Sherry's kitchen, a couple of days after we found out that Porkchop had died in the fire. Dad was there too. And I had asked him, "Do you think that woman at the dog park was right?"

Those were the first words I'd spoken all day. I couldn't talk about my dog. I couldn't think about our house, about all our books and my parents' old photo albums and my stuffies. And Porkchop. Porkchop. Porkchop. I couldn't let any of that into my head for more than a couple of seconds. When those thoughts burst in, it got hard to move, hard to even breathe. The only thing that I could do was think about what Dog-Park Laura had said about the tar sands being responsible for the wildfire. She'd given me something to blame for all we'd lost.

Dad looked at me blankly, so I reminded him how the woman had blamed the wildfire on the tar sands. He and Mom were both on autopilot, going through the motions of eating and showering and sleeping. They were supposed to be looking for a condo or a house to rent, and a school where I could finish grade ten, but they couldn't seem to manage much more than getting out of bed each morning. I was no different. At least not until I asked that question.

Dad shrugged. "Do I think she's right? Probably."

Probably was all I needed to hear.

I took my phone outside to Auntie Sherry's back deck. The sun was still shining, even though it was eight at night. The long summer days, still getting longer. My eyes burned with the smoke that was flowing south from Fort Mac; I could smell the smoke in my hair, in my clothes.

I googled Premier Nancy Reese, her official government page providing a neat rectangle of space where I could type a message. She looked so warm, so kind, with her silver-white hair and purple glasses. I liked her. I trusted her. So I wrote what I thought, what I felt. I wanted an answer. I wanted her to understand and to do something. To fix things.

"Dear Premier Nancy: The Fort McMurray fire killed my dog, Porkchop. What if Fort Mac had run on solar panels instead of tar? What if carbon from the tar sands hadn't dried our forests to a crisp? Would Porkchop still be alive? She was the sweetest dog imaginable, and you owe it to her to stop the tar sands. Do it for her. And for all of us."

I felt a buzzing mix of hope and relief when I clicked send. It felt comforting to speak out. To tell one powerful person how I felt.

And if telling one person made me feel a little better, telling everyone would help even more.

I cut out enough characters to put the letter on Twitter, adding the hashtag #TarSandsKilledMyDog. Stupid, stupid, stupid me.

When I checked Twitter the next afternoon, I noticed the numbers first.

2,314 comments on my tweet.

313 retweets

I scrolled down through the waves of comments, more and more popping up by the second. People were calling me all sorts of mean things: childish, un-Albertan, unfair, ecoterrorist, a stain on the province. But two comments, one right after the other, froze my entire body.

> @piss88 Her dog died? Guess the wrong bitch burned. Let's fix that.

> @rayoflight One bitch down, one to go

I dropped my phone on Auntie Sherry's tiled kitchen floor. The screen shattered and parts of me did too. I still see those two tweets flash through my brain almost every day. And that wasn't even the worst of it. That was still to come.

And here, now, ten months later, while I'm looking at Renzi's GreenAída tweets, this weird noise escapes from my mouth — a gurgle of sadness and fear and frustration. I know Renzi's completely right about everything she's saying. I feel exactly the same way she does. But I am so, so scared about how people will respond to her. How they might threaten her the way they threatened me. My hand flies up to that spot on my head.

"Davis! Stop scratching!" Mom swats my hand away from my scalp. "If you don't stop that soon, I'm taking you to see Dr. Patel and getting you on those anxiety meds we've talked about."

"Mom, I'm fine," I say, rolling my eyes as I swallow some water and regain control over myself. "It's just a stupid habit."

"Or lice," Dad says, smiling.

"It's not lice." I fake laugh, desperately trying to set my Mom at ease. "It's just that one spot."

"A louse, then."

Sure. Let's go with that. Please.

JAE

Jae is manoeuvring her second contact lens into place when her phone starts ringing. She scrambles to answer, unused to the sound of an incoming phone call instead of a text.

"Come upstairs to my office, please," her mother says through the phone. "I need to discuss one of the emails you sent me."

Her mother hangs up before Jae can respond. There's so much wrong with what just transpired. The fact that her mother phoned her rather than coming downstairs or even just yelling. The fact that her mother summoned her like a servant. The fact that her mother didn't bother to say hello or good morning.

All facts aside, Jae smiles and hugs herself as she hurries upstairs. She had forwarded her mother a bunch of emails from different Canadian vet schools, each of which confirmed that it would be fine for Jae to get her undergrad science degree in animal health at the University of Alberta instead of the University of Toronto. Her mom must have read the messages. And, hopefully, she'll agree to let Jae stay here next year instead of moving to Toronto.

Jae rushes into her mother's office, the entire third floor of their massive house. Jae almost never comes up here, and so she's struck every time by the incredible view of the surrounding Haven Ravine. So many trees. And even more birds.

"This video you sent me," Jae's mother says, not looking up from her screen, "do you think many of your classmates have seen it?" Heather Schmidt is dressed in her standard navy power suit, a pearl necklace in place to soften the look. She must have an online meeting, or something, to still be home at this hour. Her hair is pulled back into a perfect French twist, the opposite of Jae's loose, flyaway waves. She turns her monitor toward Jae and presses play.

The video is shot from a plane, and it looks like they're flying over some horrible, barren planet. Where Jae knows there had probably once been trees and green, there is only scraped earth. All that's alive and healthy has been chewed away, with trails of frothy yellow slime and black-brown slicks left behind.

It's the enormity of it that stuns Jae the most, even though she's watched this video at least twenty times. You can see tiny trucks way down below, smaller than little kids' toys, chugging up and down roads and pits. The voice narrating the video explains that those trucks are as big as houses, so tall that their drivers need ladders to get into them.

Jae did indeed send the video to her mother, but that was over a year ago. The video was made by Izzy's older sister, Dr. Nakita Malone, as a protest against the Fort Mac tar sands. Jae sent it to her mother right after the winter formal dance in grade eleven. She needed a way to shut down any encouragement from her mother to see Izzy again, and she figured proof of his genetic connection to the province's most outspoken environmental activist would do the trick.

Too bad her mother probably hadn't watched the video until now.

"Well, Jae? I haven't got all morning. How well known is this video among your peers?"

"Uh," Jae says. She really doesn't know. Anyone within earshot of Izzy has probably heard of it, as the guy constantly talks about his sister and her awesomeness. Izzy is so clearly trying to get out from under his sister's shadow. Or maybe glom onto her notoriety. But it's impossible to say how many kids actually went and watched the video after hearing Izzy talk about it.

"I tracked down the pilot," Jae's mother says. "It turns out he offered to fly this Nakita woman over the nearby reclamation areas, to show her the areas that had been replanted, instead of only flying over the active mine. But she refused. Do you think that knowing the full story would impact teens who've seen this video? Would it make them see this video as propaganda?"

Jae scrunches up her face. "Maybe? I mean, no one wants to feel they've been manipulated, right?"

Heather Schmidt nods and gives Jae a quick smile. "Good. That's really useful information."

Jae feels a rush of happiness. It's nice to feel needed. Useful.

"That's all I need from you. It helps me understand the sixteen- to eighteen-year-old demographic. Thank you," her mother says.

Heather Schmidt doesn't say "you're dismissed," but that's what Jae hears. Jae has often wondered why her mother even bothered to have her. Why she went through the trouble of finding a sperm donor and a fertility clinic. Her mother must have foreseen that she would one day require insight into the teenage demographic to help her get ahead at work.

"Did you have a chance to read through the emails I sent you this week? About me maybe going to the U of A rather than the U of T?"

Keeping her eyes on her computer screen and typing as she talks, Heather Schmidt says, "Don't be foolish, Jae. The University of Toronto is Canada's top-ranked school, and you are very lucky that I was able to secure a spot there despite your late application."

"But —"

"You know I only want the best for you. Have a good day at school, Jae."

Jae turns and leaves the office, silent and deflated. She remembers the last time her mom ended a conversation with those exact same words. It was way back when Jae was thirteen, and she had confided in her mother. The first person Jae had told the biggest truth about herself.

"Don't be ridiculous," her mother had snapped. "What you are is thirteen. Have a good day at school."

What you are is thirteen.

As if thirteen were too young to know.

DAVIS

I'm just getting out of the shower when Mom starts dropping f-bombs, and I hear slamming drawers and hangers crashing into each other. I race out of the bathroom in my towel, my hair still dripping wet.

Crap. The bruises on my legs are exposed. I run back to the bathroom, dry my legs and throw on my pants as I shout, "Mom? Are you okay? What's going on?"

I run to her room as soon as I'm dressed. Mom's standing in front of her closet in dress pants and her bra, flinging through her clothes like they've committed some heinous crime against her. As soon as she gets to the last shirt, she starts rifling through them in the opposite direction.

"It's Green Shirt Day at work, and I cannot for the life of me find my green sweater. I'm already late, but HR made it *very* clear that they want us all dressed in green to show our environmental commitment. Greenwearing is the new greenwashing, for God's sake." She reaches the last sweater and then storms over to her chest of drawers. Shirts and sweaters go flying through the air like she's a raging twelve-year-old having a meltdown.

I open a drawer on the opposite side of her and start digging. "Which sweater do you mean?"

She slams a drawer shut and starts yanking curlers from her hair. "That emerald green one. It's the only green thing I have. You know it — it's the wool one that's always covered in Porkchop's hair."

We both freeze when she says our dog's name. That's why she can't find the sweater. It didn't survive the Fort Mac fire. Mom looks like she's going to burst into tears. "Wait right here," I say. "I have something."

I run to my room and fling through the piles of books and papers and dirty clothes strewn across my floor. The sparkle catches my eye. Found it! I race back to Mom and show her the beautiful green scarf that Jae and Renzi gave me that day at Red Caboose. I drape the scarf around Mom's shoulders and lightly around her neck. It's perfect.

"You'll need a shirt underneath, though," I tease gently as Mom runs her hand across the fabric. Mom wipes her thumbs under her eyes and yanks on a turtleneck before rearranging the scarf.

"This is lovely, Davis. Thank you. You saved the day. Again. I've gotta run. Have a good day, sweetheart." She kisses me on the head and then hurries to leave.

"MOM!" I shout. She stops and turns around, startled. "You still have three curlers in your hair!" I run to her and pull them out.

She pulls me into a tight hug, and I am pretty sure she's thinking about Porkchop, just like I am. Maybe, just maybe, she's also thinking that she should quit working for Haus Oil and its stupid pipeline project.

Probably not. But maybe.

I've already missed the 8:30 bus by the time I finish breakfast, so I grab my bike, even though it's one thousand and eight degrees below zero. And will probably start snowing at any second. You'd think winter should be ending by now, but it just drags on and on and on.

Ella is leaning against my locker when I finally get into school, frozen and covered in snow but also feeling proud of myself for biking without crashing.

"What happened to you?" Ella asks, her eyes wide. "Your face is bright red and your hair looks wet. You didn't walk, did you? You know I could have picked you up, right? And — " Ella leans in, her lips so glossy that the glare from the overhead lights is almost blinding — "is that thing in your nose infected?"

"Nah," Ben says from a few lockers down. "Fake nose pus is totally the latest trend. Didn't you know that, Ella?"

"Totally," I say. "Grabbed a big spoonful of honey, mixed in some green food colouring and slathered it all on." I try to reach my nose with my tongue. "Bonus points because it tastes so yummy."

"Gross, Davis," Ella says, wincing as she closes her locker.

Ben rolls his eyes, and I want to hug him. He's wearing that fake sports jersey I adore, the one that says "Sports Team Name Here" and "Sports Icon Name Here" on the back. Why can't I be crazily in love with him in all his freckly glory? My life would be so much easier if my heart could be as rational as my brain. I throw my dripping coat, bike helmet and drenched backpack into my locker and slam it shut, waving a quick goodbye to Ben.

You know, the guy who always responds to my texts.

I stomp all the way to French, punching my leg as I walk. Pow. Pow. Pow. I plop myself down into my desk and dig out my phone, pulling up my text history with Izzy and composing a new one.

Davis: Is your sister Nakita accepting new patients?

I get a rush when I click the green send arrow, a thrill of energy and joy and hope. And then I crash. Just like an addict. An Izzy addict. What a stupid, stupid thing to text. If I really wanted to know the answer, I would have just called her clinic. Obviously, I am a stalker. Obviously, I just wanted to text Izzy.

Again.

But, in my defence, it is true that I desperately want to meet Dr. Nakita Malone.

She's even more badass than Renzi. My favourite YouTube video shows Nakita standing in front of an image of an open pit tar sands mine, the land scraped down to the point that it looks like the moon. I've watched the clip so many times that I know Nakita's words by heart: "Our province's tar sands are the largest industrial extraction project on the planet. They are the biggest industrial source of carbon emissions in the country, and one of the biggest on this beautiful, fragile planet." And then she goes on to list all sorts of different actions a person could take: pulling their money from banks that invest in fossil fuels, occupying your school or workplace, staging a Die-in outside companies like Haus. I don't really know what a Die-in is, but I'm sure Izzy does. So I text him and ask him. I know that he won't believe that I'd ever plan something like that, so I hurriedly text Jae and Renzi to say that I think we should organize a Die-in. Just to make it real. Bringing them in on my idea calms me a little, but not much.

And then, as soon as French class ends, I text Izzy again.

> **Davis:** I want to meet Nakita because of all her activist work. Not just because she's your sister.

No. No. No. Why did I send that? I'm so, so stupid. Completely out of control. I rush down the hall and drop myself down by Renzi and Jae's lockers, burying my face in my knees.

"Why so blue, amiga?" Renzi asks as she and Jae lower themselves down beside me.

"Because I'm a monumental doofus. I sent a text to Izzy that I definitely should not have sent. Followed by another that tried to explain the previous one. Followed by one last one, trying to fix the one I sent to try to fix the first one." I hold my phone out far from my body. "Someone please take this from me. I cannot be trusted with it."

"We've all done stuff like this." Jae's voice is low and soothing. Her hand is on my knee. "We've all said things we've regretted. Heck, I had to get on my knees and apologize to Renzi because I said something mean the other day. Don't beat yourself up."

My breath catches in my throat. How does she know about the punches? Can she see the bruises through my jeans? Or has she seen me throw a punch or two? (Or twelve?)

"Seriously," Renzi adds. "You're way too hard on yourself."

Oh. Right. That kind of beating yourself up. Got it.

"Now, what was this thing you texted about a Die-in?" Renzi asks.

I shake my head, my face still buried in my knees. "Even if I organize a Die-in, if I ever figure out what that even is, I'm not sure that will win Izzy back. What if he had totally different reasons for dumping me that have nothing to do with the fact that I'm a climate wuss? I mean, I know he's hardcore, but I can't help but think there's something more. Do you think he likes someone else?"

"Renzi," Jae says, her voice weirdly flat, "Do you have any insight into what might be going through Izzy's mind?"

Renzi startles and her water bottle flies from her hand, its purple glass shattering as it hits the concrete floor of our hallway.

"*Carajo*," Renzi exclaims.

I jump up to collect the broken bottle, its fractured fragments held in place by the bottle's silicone shell. I hand the bottle back to Renzi, worried that I'm going to accidentally cut her. She shakes her head and points at the trash can. She's right — there can be no salvaging the bottle.

"Carajo," Renzi repeats, smacking Jae's shoulder lightly. "That was my absolute favourite water bottle."

There's something going on here, something that I need to fix. Immediately. "Are you guys mad? I didn't mean to talk so much about Izzy —"

Renzi claps her hands together, the smacking sound silencing me immediately. "Enough! No guy talk allowed. There are way more interesting and important things to discuss."

Jae rolls her eyes and makes a loud, exasperated sigh.

"It's okay, Jae. Don't be angry. Renzi's right. The world is on fire, and this pipeline is about to make the fire so much worse. It's going to, like, triple production in the tar sands. I shouldn't waste my time stressing about some stupid guy." A badass wouldn't do that. Renzi wouldn't do that.

I expect Renzi to ignore what I've said and keep arguing with Jae, to defend herself and escalate the argument, but Renzi does the exact opposite. She shakes her head slowly and wraps her arms around herself. "Oh, nena. Stressing about stupid guys is more common than you'd think. Especially when a stupid guy gets in between you and the friends you treasure more than anything else."

Is that what Renzi thinks, that I'm letting Izzy get between me, her and Jae? Or maybe she's talking about her ex-boyfriend, that Camilo Fuentes guy. Part of me wants to ask, but mostly I just want to change the subject. Immediately.

Before I can say anything, Jae intervenes. She puts her hand on my arm and squeezes. "The heart wants what it wants, Davis." Her voice is warm again. "No matter how much you wish it didn't."

"Too true," Renzi says, tapping Jae's foot with hers. "Too true."

RENZI

Reggaetón is blasting so loudly inside the Red Caboose that Renzi doesn't hear him come in. She doesn't see him either, as she's focused on pricing the latest batch of clothes that need to go out on the racks.

But she sure smells him. The telltale minty wallop of a guy fixated on the smell of his own breath.

"*Buenas tardes, hermosa*," Izzy says, bowing as he approaches the counter. Good afternoon, beautiful. Or, at least, Renzi thinks that's what he's trying to say. His consonants are so harsh, the vowels all wrong and the "h" so not silent that it's hard to tell.

Renzi loves her Island family, but she hates how her cousins tease her about her Spanish, correcting her grammar as though she were a toddler. And she can't stand how her uncles refer to her absent dad as *El Gringo Chino*, as if his American-ness or his Chinese-ness were the obvious sources of his assholeish-ness. That said, the Zángano's horrible Gringo Spanish is still utterly intolerable.

"I'm working, Izzy," Renzi says, keeping her eyes focused on the clothes in front of her. This is only the third time she's ever been alone with him. The first was back in September when she launched the Climate Club about a week before the first hurricane hit. At first, only Jae had shown up, but then Izzy had strutted into the classroom, plopped himself on top of one of the desks and launched into a monologue about climate change. It was all stuff Renzi knew, stuff she actually understood way better than Izzy. It was obnoxious to be lectured at, but damn, he was cute. The gaze between the two of them was unbroken, the energy passing between them palpable. Jae had raced out of the classroom almost immediately, leaving Izzy and Renzi alone.

Izzy had asked Renzi out a few days later, but the first hurricane hit the Island right before his text came in. She never answered. He kept texting, though, and asked her out again around Halloween and again in late November. She'd said no both times, explaining that she was still preoccupied by the hurricanes and not ready to date anyone.

The second time Renzi and Izzy were alone was right before Valentine's Day. The night she screwed up and made out with him. The night he dumped Davis. The night Renzi would really rather forget.

Izzy slides his phone into Renzi's line of sight. On the screen, a list of math classes running next fall at the University of Alberta. She recognizes them right away because she is registered in three of them.

"I know you're doing honours math next year," Izzy says, leaning forward so his forehead is almost touching Renzi's. "So tell me which of these you're taking, and I'll join you. I'll probably need mucho tutoring help." He wiggles his eyebrows and grins. Those curls, those sideburns, those kissable lips and those broad shoulders — Renzi knows that Izzy is well aware of just how hot he is. It's highly unlikely that he's equally aware of how aggravating he is.

Renzi wants to scream, but she doesn't want to give the Zángano the satisfaction of knowing he gets under her skin. "I thought you were majoring in computer science." She's careful not to phrase it as a question. The sooner this conversation ends, the better.

"And minoring in math," he says. He rests his chin in his hand, apparently in no hurry to leave. "It's okay if you don't want to tell me yet. I know you'll come around eventually. Sooner or later, you will fall madly in love with me. It's inevitable. One more question, though: What city do your grandparents live in? Mom and Dad took Nakita and me on a family vacation to Cuba when she graduated high school, so I want them to take me to Puerto Rico for my grad present. And there's no way I'm going there without meeting your peeps."

Renzi gathers up all the clothes from the counter with one quick swipe of her arms. She marches out from behind the counter and pushes past Izzy, saying nothing. Her face is hot, throbbing with anger and frustration. He just doesn't stop. He just doesn't know when to stop. Or if he knows, he doesn't care. It got really out of control over the Christmas break when she was on the Island with Lino and Mami. He had texted her daily during the first days of the trip, his texts increasing in frequency and desperation the longer she went without responding.

And then he'd started calling.

And calling and calling and calling.

Finally, Lino had grabbed Renzi's phone, holding it high above his head, out of her reach. "Either you answer this poor fool's calls, or I will do it for you."

She'd taken the easy path and just blocked Izzy's number. It was so simple to do, and it allowed her to focus on her grandparents and fixing up their house post-hurricane. Once she blocked Izzy, it was much easier to enjoy the Island's humid air and the music and the perfect ocean water.

She loves how at ease she feels in Puerto Rico, the one place on earth where she has more to learn than to prove. And she absolutely adores her abuelos. And her tíos and tías and most of her cousins. They are such fighters, so determined to make things better for the Island, so dedicated to pressing for change.

And stupid Izzy Malone thinks he can and should be part of that? No. *Absolutamente no.*

"Izzy," Renzi finally says, struggling to keep her voice calm, struggling not to yell. "I have work to do. You need to leave, okay? Now."

She doesn't look at him. Doesn't check to see if he is smiling or frowning or pressing his full lips together. She just waits for him to leave. And he does, telling her his Hardware Depot shift is starting anyway. Telling her that he is a patient man and willing to wait as long as he needs to.

"Carajo!" Renzi curses as soon as the store's door closes behind Izzy. Carajo and carajo and carajo again.

JAE

Sitting in the Edmonton Public Library with her chem notes in front of her and Kat beside her, Jae has two big realizations:

1. Just because someone is fourteen months older and already in university, that doesn't mean they actually understand chemistry better than you do.
2. It is really, really difficult to study for a chemistry exam when your knee keeps brushing up against the leg of the hottest tutor of all time.

Kat clears her throat. "So, Jae," she says quietly, "what can you tell me about the rules of chemical attraction?"

Jae frowns and flips the pages in her binder. "I don't think that's on the test." She turns and looks at Kat, a little panicky. Kat is smiling.

Oh. Got it. Jae grabs her periodic table and finds what she's looking for. "That was tellurium, arsenic, indium and, um, gluon, right?"

Now it's Kat's turn to frown. Jae draws the elements on her page.

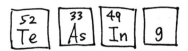

Kat bursts out laughing, bringing a dirty look from the guy at the table in front of them. "Sorry," Kat says, holding up her hand. "Seriously, though, Jae. Are you going out with someone? Do you like anyone?"

Jae looks at the table again, staring at the atomic numbers 39, 8 and 92.

She doesn't have the guts to say that one, though. Not yet. Not quite. "I've never really dated anyone. I have only kissed exactly one person, and I don't think there's anyone on the planet I like less than him. Gross, gross, gross."

"Why?" Kat asks quietly. "If you kissed him, he couldn't be that bad, could he?"

Jae shrugs. There are certainly worse guys at school. Guys who are ruder, cruder and a lot less smart. Jae brushes her hand up against Kat's. "I dunno. Maybe I just hate him because I only went out with him to make my mother happy. And I really, really hate that I let him kiss me. Because" — she bites her lip, takes a deep meditative breath — "because he's a guy. And that's not really who I'm into."

Kat links her pinkie finger with Jae's. "Oh? Who are you into?"

Jae takes another big, deep breath. With her free hand, she points to the letters on the periodic table.

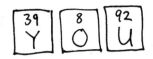

DAVIS

I punch my leg and then press Command + P on my laptop, printing the anti-pipeline flyer. (And yes, I think about the trees; I am printing on scrap paper I collected from school. So there.)

"Your school phoned today," I imagine Mom saying, her voice thick with concern. "The call sent me right back to that day last year with your principal. You need to be careful, sweetheart."

Or maybe it would go down another way.

"Davis? Did you make this?" Izzy will ask. Then he will run up to me, pick me up in his arms, spin me around and kiss me.

Or maybe some hater will grab the poster from my hand, crumple it into a ball and shove it down my throat.

Or maybe I won't even get caught. I won't get Izzy's attention, I won't change anyone's mind, and I won't accomplish anything more than wasting paper, ink and my new friends' time.

You know who I should ask? Ben.

I snap a picture of my flyer and send it to him.

Davis: Like it?
Davis: I'm gonna put a copy on every truck
and SUV windshield in the school parking lot.

His reply is immediate.

Ben: U don't want to do that, D.

He's right. Of course he's right. He doesn't have to remind me about what happened the last time I spoke out against fossil fuels.

Ben: Do I have to remind u about what happened
  last time?
Ben: And this province totally depends on oil and gas.
Ben: And on the oil sands.
Ben: We need that pipeline.
Ben: Over and out.

Ben's texts bang back and forth in my mind as Jae, Renzi and I head toward the parking lot at lunch. The words themselves aren't surprising — living in Alberta, you hear that kind of stuff every day. The thing that completely knocks me to the ground and jumps all over my brain is that those words came from Ben.

Because Ben and I agree about EVERYTHING.

That dessert peanut butter — with all its sugar and creepily consistent texture — is a crime against real peanut butter.

That Jay-Z is overrated.

That *Star Trek* is eminently superior to *Star Wars*.

That Philip K. Dick was more creative than Shakespeare.

So the fact that Ben and I completely, fundamentally

disagree about the pipeline just does not compute. Ben is not a redneck. He is not ill-informed. He is a total sweetheart, and he is worried about climate change. How is it possible that we haven't talked about the pipeline before?

I mean, I know Ben's brother works in Fort Mac. Dad still does too. But I never once imagined that Ben would think the tar sands are a good thing.

And he was so sweet to me that horrible day last year, so kind and supportive. And he's been the only real friend I've had here up until Renzi and Jae came into my life. Definitely more of a friend to me than Emma or Ella. Or even Izzy, if I'm completely honest. How could that same great person be totally on the side of the oil industry?

"It's not like we're slashing tires, amiguita," Renzi says when I voice all of my fears as we walk through the school parking lot. She grabs a bunch of flyers from my hands and shoves one under the wind-shield wiper of the first truck we see.

> There is no **Planet B**.
> Oil and gas **do not** love you back.
>
> ## STOP THE HAUS PIPELINE
> @GreenAída

Jae walks along beside us, a stack of flyers in her hands. One windshield after another is papered with our protest.

Then, from our left, an angry shout. "What the fuck did you put on my truck?"

A hulking grade-twelve guy in a football jacket and base-ball cap charges toward us, a crumpled flyer in his hands. Rage radiates from him. And right then, right in that punch of fear, I am hurled ten months back in time, into the eye of the HateStorm.

It was June 18, last year.

I stood in front of my new locker at Strathearn, just as lunch was ending, surprised by the puffy goldenrod envelope taped to my locker's blue metal door. The envelope had my name on it, and my heart started pounding. I'd always dreamed about getting a love letter from a secret admirer. It was almost enough to make me temporarily forget Porkchop's death and the terror of escaping the Fort Mac fire just weeks before.

"Did you see who put this here?" I asked the freckly, blue-eyed kid at a locker near mine. Ben Cron, I would later learn. It's so weird that I didn't even know his name then. He just shrugged and shook his head.

I pulled the envelope off my locker, trying to remove the tape without tearing the package. I slid my finger inside the upper seal and gently pried it open.

I looked inside, expecting a book of poetry or a letter or a rose. Instead, I found a piece of meat and bone, charred almost beyond recognition. It was a badly burned pork chop. There was no note, but a note wasn't needed. I got the message, loud and clear.

I dropped the package like it was on fire, my hands flying up to my mouth to stifle a scream. Images of my sweet, silly dog running and drooling and licking my face raced through my mind, only to be pushed out by imagined scenes of her choking on thick smoke and burning. And just as the thick envelope landed at my feet, I heard my name called over the intercom system.

"Davis Klein-Mah to the office, please."

I froze, panic gluing me in place. This wasn't my fault. I hadn't done anything wrong. Someone had made an evil, twisted joke about Porkchop, so why was I in trouble?

"Davis Klein-Mah to the office."

It was only when Ben put his hand on my shoulder and asked me if I was okay that I managed to move. One foot in front of the other, Ben by my side, I made my way to the office. Part of me knew I should take the envelope, hold onto it as proof (of what, I wasn't sure), but I couldn't touch it. I didn't even want to look at it.

When I turned the corner to the main office, I saw my parents standing there with Mr. McNally, the principal. How did they know about the envelope with the burned pork chop? They couldn't know. A thousand billion questions rushed through my brain as I hurried toward them.

Mr. McNally saw me first, his big brown eyes fuzzy behind his thick glasses. He waved me forward, kindly. Gently. Mom and Dad turned, and then rushed toward me.

"Let's talk in my office," Mr. McNally said.

"How did you find out? Did you get packages too?" I asked before Mr. McNally had even closed his office door. Mom had her arm around my shoulder; Dad had my hand in his. The puzzled looks that passed between the three adults told me they had no idea what I was talking about.

And so I had to explain. When I saw Mr. McNally's confusion, I told him that Porkchop was my dog, and that I was the girl who wrote that infamous tweet.

Mr. McNally took off his glasses and rubbed his eyes. Red streaks were rushing up his cheeks and across his bald head.

"Let me assure you, Davis, I will find out who did this. And there will be consequences. Serious ones. Let me also assure you that you are, and will be, safe in this school."

Mom wiped her eyes; Dad did the same.

"But I don't understand," I protested. "If you didn't know about the envelope, the burned pork chop, then what's going on?"

Mr. McNally cleared his throat, returned his glasses to his face. "I got a disturbing phone call this morning, Davis. And I thought it best to contact your parents immediately." He looked from me to Mom and Dad. "The safety of our students is my number one priority, and I cannot tolerate threats of any kind."

I let out a strangled gasp of air, a sound of shock and fear and confusion. Mom pulled me toward her and kissed my head. "Someone phoned Principal McNally, sweetheart. A funeral home. They were calling to arrange a memorial service at the school."

The memorial service was supposed to be for me.

"It was a sick, cruel joke, sweetie," Dad said, squeezing my hand.

Mr. McNally wanted to call a school assembly to denounce the threats, but I refused. More attention was the last thing I wanted.

Mom and Dad made me start seeing Jolene, the therapist who was all about cyberbullying and guarding my online privacy. Such a waste of time and of Haus Oil's benefits plan. All I wanted was to forget that any of this had happened. To bury any and all recollections of the threats and the hate and the evil, pushing it down and down and down until it would no longer haunt me. But the harder you try to forget something, the deeper that something sinks its claws into every piece of you.

"I said," the angry grade twelve guy shouts again, yanking me back to the present, "what the fuck did you put on my truck?"

Terror courses through me and a small burst of vomit rushes into my mouth. I take a panicky step backward and land a couple of hard punches on my legs. Before I can hit myself again, Jae wraps her arms around me from behind in a tight hug.

"Are you okay?" she whispers in my ear.

I nod and then whisper out a yes, but Jae keeps holding on. I am so grateful, I almost start crying.

Renzi looks at me, the worry evident on her face. She seems to hesitate for a moment but then she steps forward, flipping her purple curls over her shoulder. "I believe it's a flyer. Do you need some help reading the words?"

"Go to hell," the guy shouts, throwing the crumpled flyer at Renzi. "And stay away from my truck."

Renzi turns to Jae and me, shrugging. "That went well." And then she puts a flyer under the wiper of another truck.

RENZI

"I think we should have an intervention with Davis," Jae says while Renzi closes up Red Caboose for the day. Renzi powers down the computer and sends her boss a text about how the shift went. "Tell her how worried we are about all the head scratching and leg hitting and stuff. And about all those texts she keeps sending Izzy."

Renzi pulls on her coat, trying to figure out how best to respond. She agrees but also doesn't. Maybe this is the moment to tell Jae what she's been thinking and wondering and talking to Mami about, without getting all up in Jae's business. Without making Jae uncomfortable or pressuring her. Renzi lifts her curls off her neck and twists them into a bun that quickly unravels.

Without looking at Jae, Renzi says, "I don't know, amiga. I'm really worried too, but I've been reading a lot about boundaries. About asking friends questions that they might not be ready to answer. Most of the articles say not to press, to just be supportive and wait for your friend to share her truth when she's ready. What do you think?" There. She said it. Without actually saying it. Which is the opposite of how Renzi usually makes her way forward in the world.

"Boundaries," Jae says, frowning. She follows Renzi to the door. "Maybe you're right. I don't know. But we should tell her about you and Izzy. She's going to find out eventually, and she should hear it from you."

What? This was not the conversation Renzi wanted to have. She turns the key in the store lock, struggling to keep her voice steady. "What do you mean about me and Izzy? There is no me and Izzy. You know I'd never go out with someone my very best friend cannot stand. Just like you know I'd never go out with someone who mansplains climate change to me, even if he is hotter than hot. You know that." Renzi hates how quickly she's talking. She hates how defensive she sounds. The opposite of believable.

"Renz," Jae says as they walk out to the parking lot, "of course I know you wouldn't go out with Izzy. You wouldn't do that. I just mean that you should tell Davis that Izzy is totally in love with you. That he's asked you out a dozen times and that he gave you, like, a thousand dollars for that generator. He obviously dumped Davis because he's fixated on you."

Caramba. Jae doesn't even know the half of it.

There was a day way back in January when Renzi had dragged Jae out to the End of the World. Jae had noticed that there weren't any chickadees or magpies or sparrows in sight, and she joked that the birds were respecting the No Trespassing signs. But when they reached the end of the path, both girls saw that they were not alone. Izzy was sitting on the retaining wall, his arms wrapped around Davis.

Renzi had cracked a joke about how Izzy clearly had a type because Davis is half Chinese like Renzi.

But Jae had just shaken her head. "That poor, poor girl," she'd said. "She's cute, but she's definitely not you. I see nothing but heartbreak in that one's future."

Jae had called it then. But how would Jae react when she found out that Izzy had dumped Davis with a text right in front of Renzi, immediately after they'd kissed? Not well. Not well at all. There's a solid chance that Jae will blame Renzi and that kiss for the fact that Davis is spinning out of control. And Jae won't be wrong.

"Secrets will eat you from the inside," Jae says as she and Renzi get into her Tesla. "Chewing and gnawing at you. Keeping things secret gives them too much strength. Too much power."

Renzi feels tears starting to well up.

Jae looks over at Renzi and gives her a small smile. Something in Jae's eyes seems to soften. "Before we say anything to Davis about Izzy, though, we might want to say something about that honking thing in her nose. Friends should not let friends wear something like that."

Renzi laughs. She leans her head against the Tesla's headrest, relieved. "I haven't said anything about her nose stud either. Boundaries, privacy, blah blah blah. But caramba, I keep waiting for her nostril to stage an uprising. To take its revenge and free Davis from the tyranny of that awful thing."

Jae's phone warbles, and she checks it as soon as they hit a red light.

"It's Davis," Jae reports. "She wants to know if we can meet her at the Hardware Depot on Gateway Boulevard in thirty minutes. That's random."

No. It isn't. It's the opposite of random.

Renzi knows exactly who works at that Hardware Depot. Exactly whom Davis must be trying to see.

"Oh no," Renzi whispers, too quietly for Jae to hear.

Oh no, oh no, oh no.

DAVIS

I have a good reason for being here.

Really.

A reason that has nothing to do with Izzy Malone.

Really.

I push the shopping cart up and down the aisles of Hardware Depot, trying to look like I'm doing something other than searching for Izzy in his orange apron. Maybe he doesn't even work here anymore. I pull a box of screws from the shelf and place them in my empty cart. Dad probably has enough screws and nails in his workshop, but it would be terrible to run out, right? And I'm going to need plywood. Lots of it.

I can use Dad's drill and his hammer and his saw. And when I accidentally chop off my arm, I will finally have a legitimate reason for going to see Dr. Nakita Malone.

I turn the cart toward the paint section, knowing Izzy sometimes works there.

"Davis?" he will say, the look on his face a mixture of annoyance and dread.

I will raise my eyebrows at him and flip my hair over my shoulder, silently communicating that I am definitely NOT here to see him. As I push past him, not stopping to say hello, Izzy will grab my elbow.

We will stand there, glaring at one another, and then I will coolly explain that I'm building a tiny house in the path of Haus's Trans-Provincial Pipeline, just like the Tiny House Warriors in Secwepemc Indigenous territory across the Alberta/B.C. border are doing.

"Davis, that's, that's —"

My heart will thud, pounding blood through my body, as I wait for the remainder of his sentence. The words that will follow will be some combination of "amazing" or "brilliant" or "*seriously* badass."

"That's cultural appropriation."

Damn it. Even my imagination has turned against me.

Of course it's cultural appropriation. Izzy schooled me in cultural appropriation dozens of times, but I guess his lessons haven't fully sunk in. Of course he'll call me out for it.

I've been spending loads of time reading about the incredible anti-pipeline protest actions being led by Indigenous people. It isn't just the Standing Rock Sioux and the fight against the Dakota Access pipeline. It's the fight for clean drinking water, and the fight against the Energy East Pipeline. And now the fight is against Haus, the very same company that pays Mom's and Dad's salaries.

Sure, not all Indigenous people are against the pipeline. Some have spoken out about needing the jobs and the revenue. But there's a lot more Indigenous action against the Haus pipeline than for it. I've watched videos and read blogs and visited Facebook pages, showing Indigenous peoples signing a treaty against the tar sands, building tiny homes on the proposed pipeline routes and leading these amazing demonstrations.

It's a fight I want to be part of, but it's so hard not to dwell on how the haters shut me down with two bitch tweets, a piece of burned pork and a single phone call to my new school.

I push the memory of all that out of my brain, landing a quick couple of punches on my legs to distract myself.

Back to cultural appropriation, Davis. Focus.

I cast a furtive glance to my right, then to my left. And then over my shoulder. No one is here to see me abandon my shopping cart in the aisle and slowly back out of the store. I do my best to look casual as I walk away, quickening my steps the closer I get to the exit.

There's still time to text Jae and Renzi, to ask them not to come. To cancel the plan.

Jae: we're here!

Hand, meet forehead.

Davis: DO NOT COME!
Davis: I messed up!

I walk out to the parking lot, with no idea how to explain myself to Jae and Renzi. I'd taken the bus to the store, but I'd asked them to meet me here with Jae's car because I had this great and wonderful and brilliant surprise and would need their help to get it home. Jae and Renzi get out of Jae's Tesla when they see me, but I shake my head, holding my hands up.

"Sorry, sorry, sorry."

As soon as we are all inside Jae's car, I tell them the truth, winding my words from the tiny house plan to the cultural appropriation realization, skipping the part about trying to impress Izzy.

"And here's the horrible thing," I say, the words tumbling from my mouth, "I don't actually know a single Indigenous person. Not one, even though maybe some of the kids at school are. And that is completely unacceptable because Edmonton has a huge Indigenous population and —"

"You have to stop scratching your head, querida," Renzi interrupts quietly. She reaches out from the front seat and gently pulls my hand down. "You're going to lose your hair."

I pull my hand away from my head, mortified.

"But you'll still look beautiful when you're bald," Jae says, catching my eye in the rear-view mirror and winking.

They are so generous. I love them both — so much so that I have to tell them the full truth. "There's also a small part of me that was hoping I'd see Izzy because he works there. A teeny tiny part of me. Like, ninety-eight percent of me."

"You need to forget about that zán — that fool. Put him out of your mind! And why are you freaking out about cultural appropriation, Davis? You think Indigenous people are the only ones who care about the planet? That they are the only ones who should lead protests against oil companies? As if they don't have enough shit to deal with in this country. Trust me, fighting colonialism is exhausting work." Renzi is talking quickly and loudly, like she's even more energized than usual.

Jae lifts her chin toward the car's roof. "Oh, Renzi on

119

her moral high ground. How's the air up there, my friend?"

"Easy to breathe, amiga. Refreshing too." Renzi draws in an exaggerated breath, her nose pointed upward. "Seriously, though, Davis. You shouldn't use cultural appropriation as an excuse for doing nothing."

"Ouch." I squeeze my eyes shut, trying to find a way to explain, to make them both understand. "Actually, my excuse for doing nothing is that the last time I really took a stand and spoke my mind about the tar sands, I got all these threats. Death threats. On Twitter. At school. Someone put a burned pork chop on my locker and maybe that same person called Mr. McNally to arrange a memorial at our school. And that's what's tearing me up. I want to speak out. I really, really want to organize a Die-in or something. I really do. And not just to impress Izzy either. I want to fight this pipeline for real, but I can't. I can't go through all of that again."

Renzi and Jae just stare at me from the front seat. They've probably never heard so many words come out of me in a single day.

"Oh my God, Davis, that must have been so scary." Jae's voice is so full of concern and care, I feel a million different feelings surge — sadness and the old pulse of fear, but also this overwhelming wave of gratitude that I have these two girls in my life. That they care about me. My throat feels tight, and I'm afraid that I'll get totally taken over by the memories of those months. I slip my hand under my leg and pinch myself as hard as I can. It hurts intensely, but that's kind of the point. Not kind of, it *is* the point. That physical pain grounds me, centres me, when everything feels like it's going to swallow me up.

"Things will be different this time," Renzi says, giving me a sharp nod. She taps her fingers on Jae's dashboard, a pitter-patter that grows louder and faster, faster and louder. "Because this time, nena, you have us. We are totally and completely by your side, and we have your back. And this pipeline is getting built only over our —" Renzi pauses. If she is trying to be dramatic, it's working.

She turns back toward me, raises her eyebrows and crosses her arms into an X against her chest. "Over our dead bodies."

JAE

Jae knows something is wrong the moment she pushes open the door to her house. The combined smells of bleach and fake pine hit her nostrils, stinging her eyes and pitching her into a fit of angry coughs.

Jennylyn doesn't use those kinds of cleaning products.

Ever.

Jae races into the house, not even bothering to take off her coat or winter boots. "Jennylyn? Hello?" The blinds are all closed, another thing that Jennylyn would never do. She loves sunshine as much as Jae does.

Someone else cleaned the house. Someone who wouldn't know about that special room downstairs, and that room's precious occupants.

Her birds.

No. Please, no.

Jae takes the stairs two at a time, unable to move fast enough to outrace her fears. And as she rounds the curve of the staircase into the basement, she sees the worst possible thing: the door to her birds' room is wide open and an industrial-sized fan is positioned in the doorway, blowing at maximum speed.

Jae knocks the fan right over as she scrambles into the room. Her girls are gone.

No birds, no cages, not even a stray feather. Just the overwhelming smell of bleach. She turns from the room and runs, shouting, hoping that whoever did this is still within earshot. Hoping that her girls might still be alive. That she could rescue them again.

But the house is empty.

She runs out the back door. It's freezing out — too cold to be anywhere other than inside. But Jae doesn't even notice. She scans the enormous backyard and sees nothing.

Nothing.

The garbage cans. Maybe. She races to the spot behind the garage where they keep the cans. She yanks the lid off of one can, relieved to find it empty. But when she takes the lid from the second, she howls.

The birds' empty cage is inside.

But where are her poor, poor girls?

They are still too injured to fly, too vulnerable. She should have taken them to the Wild Earth Animal Rescue. Taken them to Kat. She should have never risked caring for them at home. Jae looks around frantically, listening for Lala's sweet song, searching for a glimpse of Bertie's shimmery purple feathers or a whiff of Broke Beak's signature scent.

Maybe they're okay. Maybe they're stronger than Jae thinks. Maybe —

They are not.

Jae runs to the spruce tree at the other end of the yard, falling to her knees to scoop her girls into her arms. She cradles them against her chest, hoping they are just cold. Hoping they are just sleeping.

They are not.

None of her birds have survived the cold temperature. Still holding the birds against her chest, her entire body vibrating with rage, Jae pulls her phone from her pocket. Her call goes straight to her mother's voice mail, so she calls her mother's office.

"It's her daughter. Put me through!" Jae yells at her mom's secretary.

"I'm afraid she's in a meeting."

"It's an emergency. Get her. Now."

Jae carries her girls back to the house, holding her phone between her shoulder and her ear. She'll give them a proper burial, a nice soft blanket and a box to shelter them forever.

"Jae? What's going on?" Jae barely recognizes her mother's voice

"What happened to my birds?"

"Lower your voice, Jae. We can talk about this later. I am in the middle of a meeting."

"WHAT HAPPENED TO THEM?"

Heather Schmidt lets out a long sigh. Jae hears a shuffling, a muffled apology and the sound of a door closing. And another sigh. "The new girl phoned me to ask about them. I had no idea what she was talking about, so I told her to release them outside. Our house is not a zoo, Jae. Or a shelter."

"They all died, Mother. They. All. Died." Jae's voice is ice, her fury cold instead of hot. "And where's Jennylyn? Did you kill her too?"

"Don't be so dramatic, Jae. I fired her. She stole half my wardrobe."

Jae gasps. She hadn't seen this coming, and she should have. "No, Mom. Seriously, she didn't. I did. I sold them at the store my friend works at. Please call her and hire her back. This is my fault, not Jennylyn's."

Her mother makes a sharp, dismissive grunt. "I highly doubt that. Besides, Jennylyn was getting too demanding, and I found someone much cheaper. Now I have to get back to my meeting."

"Mom, wait! You can't fire Jennylyn! She's family!"

But Jae's mother has already ended the call.

Jae's legs crumple underneath her. She cradles her birds against her, rocking back and forth on the kitchen floor and singing her girls a final lullaby.

She calls Jennylyn, but the call goes straight to voice mail. Jae isn't sure that Jennylyn will be able to understand the apology she recorded through her hiccupy tears.

Jae is still on the floor almost an hour later when the idea strikes: she needs to do something, and fast. Something big. Something that will really get her mother's attention, show her that Jae is serious and can't just be dismissed. Or hung up on. Something more serious than just selling off her clothes.

It's going to have to be this anti-pipeline Die-in after all. Jae will just make it bigger, splashier and way, way more expensive. With her mother's credit card footing the bill.

DAVIS

I have a big French test to study for, and French is my worst subject. By far. I got an A– on the last test, but that had been a struggle, hard won through zillions of texts and video chats with Ben.

I try to memorize the grammar rules and spellings, but French just never settles down in my brain and makes itself comfortable the way math and bio and English and social studies do. So I absolutely, positively cannot allow myself to be distracted by checking my phone when I hear two texts come in, one right after the other.

I reach over and check my phone. I really hope it's Ben. A geek-out over that new *Intergalactic* series would really be welcome right now. *Qui est la plus grand Super Dork?*

Emma: Me and Ella are outside.
Ella: Come down.

I shut my eyes and groan. They will know I'm home by the light from my window. And even if they can be convinced by a text that I'm elsewhere, the ringing doorbell and the sound of Mom greeting the two girls means I'm screwed.

"Girls! It's been so long!" Mom's voice booms from downstairs. I have never, ever wondered about the genetic source of my loudness. And then Mom says the worst words imaginable: "Work has been so intense lately that I haven't been around to see you. Would you like to stay for dinner?"

I can't hear the response, but I have no doubt it was sweet and polite. And softly spoken. I groan again and head to the stairs, but Emma and Ella are already on their way up.

"Hey, stranger," Emma says, plunking herself down on my bed. Ella sits backwards on my desk chair, twisting back and forth. Like old times. And then she gets down to business. "What's going on with you?"

I shrug, trying to will this whole encounter to its conclusion. They are no doubt here to have THE TALK, the "What has happened to our friendship?" talk. The painful, awkward, unwanted talk.

"Not much," I lie. "Why? What's up?"

Emma and Ella trade a long look. I wish they'd just launch into it so that we can get this over with. It isn't that I want to break up with them, or whatever. It's just that I don't want to hang out with them anymore.

Which I guess is what breaking up means.

"You've kind of ditched us," Ella says, while Emma nods.

I shoot them a confused, baffled look. Or what I hope passes for a confused, baffled look.

"You don't eat lunch with us anymore, you don't answer our texts or do Friday rom-com night or hockey game night."

Emma sounds hurt. And I can't even protest because it's all true. I probably never even told them that the only thing I hate more than rom-coms is hockey.

Ella jumps in. "At first, I thought it was the whole Izzy thing, but that doesn't explain why you're hanging out with those grade twelve girls."

Emma shakes her head. "You're totally hooking up with Ben Cron, aren't you? A rebound fling after Izzy. You're *way* too hot for Ben, though. He's too nerdy. Too freckly. I think we need to stop this fling in its tracks. Am I right Ella?"

"So right."

I'm not even angry. All the indignation I feel about Ben — who is cute in his own sleepy-eyed, geeky way — all the irritation I feel over their visit, all of that is overpowered by relief. The shhhushers have handed me a beautiful exit strategy, a way to end our friendship without being in the wrong. I want to hoot.

"Please don't talk about Ben that way. It's not okay. Maybe you guys should just go," I say. I try my hardest to look serious, to look solemn and sad — when all I actually feel is relief.

"I told you this was a mistake," Ella says, standing.

"Really nice way to thank us, Davis." Emma's face is bright red.

No doubt Emma's talking about how nice they were to me after the fire, immediately taking me under their wings and hanging out with me all summer and into the fall, right up until I started going out with Izzy. They always included me, even when I didn't want to be included. But I'm too pissed to concede anything, so I say, "Thank you for what?"

Emma laughs, a sharp, bitter exhalation. She stands and takes a step toward me, getting right up in my face. "For what? How about for adopting you last year when everyone else at school thought you were some freak who ranted conspiracy theories on Twitter about how the oil industry killed your dog? How about staying friends with you even though you scratch your head like you desperately need to shampoo? How about for defending you when Izzy talked shit about you?"

The questions land like successive punches to the face. Actually, like a bunch of punches to the face followed by one high and powerful kick to the chest.

Ella's eyes widen. "Don't —" She puts her hand on Emma's shoulder, pulling her away from me. "Let's just go."

"What did he say?" My words are clipped and cold.

"Typical," Emma says. "We come here to try to repair our friendship, and all you care about is Izzy? Unbelievable. Come on, Ella, let's go."

But I grab Emma's wrist and hold it. "Tell me."

Emma wrenches her wrist free, an angry little smile on her face. "Liam was slamming you in the cafeteria line-up because of some anti-pipeline poster he thinks you put on his truck. Then Izzy said there was no way you could have made that poster. He said that you didn't have the balls to do something like that and that you were too busy stalking him to do anything political. And I defended you. I actually defended you."

A stalker. Izzy thinks I'm a stalker. He's calling me that. In the cafeteria. Where everyone can hear.

"What did you say to him?" My voice is a squeak.

Emma looks triumphant. I squeeze my eyes shut, preparing myself for what's coming.

"I told him to shush."

Of course she did.

As soon as they leave, I throw myself onto my bed, slamming my fists into my legs and screaming into my pillow with my heart and spirit broken all over again.

RENZI

"RENZI!"

Renzi pulls the spoon from her mouth, knowing exactly why her brother is yelling. She shoves the empty flan dish under her bed as Lino stomps down the hallway to her room. As she pushes the dish, she accidentally knocks over the new water bottle that Davis gave her this morning. "Because you broke yours," Davis had explained. "In the hallway. Remember?"

Renzi had not remembered, at least not until Davis had reminded her. Davis's replacement bottle wasn't nearly as pretty as the one Renzi had broken. But it was a thousand times more beautiful.

Lino storms into Renzi's room without knocking. "Where is it, Renzi? I made that flan for dinner with Julian tonight." Lino's voice is quiet and controlled. They are a yelling kind of family. A high-volume hollering kind of trio. If Lino isn't screaming at her, that means he is seriously pissed.

Her only option is to tell the truth.

She sets the water bottle upright and pulls the pan and spoon out from under her bed. Staring at the floor, she asks, "Have you ever cheated on a friend?"

"A *friend*? Is that what you're calling my boyfriends now? Carajo. You sound like Tía Isa."

Renzi puts her face on her knees. And she starts to cry. Actual tears. Lino sits on Renzi's bed and nudges her gently with his foot. "Spill, Renzita. What's going on?"

"It's just a stupid guy. The one who showed up with the envelope of cash right before Valentine's Day. He's the same guy who kept texting and phoning when we were on the Island. Jae hates his guts — and you know Jae, she doesn't hate *anyone*. But when he came here with all that money for the generator, we kissed, even though he was with someone else. Not Jae, but another girl. And I hate that I did that. I hate it. I even made friends with that other girl — sort of to apologize, and to make sure I'd keep myself away from him. And it turns out that I really like this girl. Way more than I ever liked the guy, and we're working on this big protest thing together, and if she finds out the truth about what I did, then I'll lose her and Jae."

"Do you have feelings for him?" Lino lowers himself onto the floor beside Renzi.

Renzi shakes her head, wipes her face with her sleeve. "No. Yes. I mean, I am stupidly, horribly attracted to him. Attracted in a way that I never even knew was possible. But he drives me berserk, and I can't stand the way he mansplains, and he doesn't listen or take no for an answer. So I guess that's a no, but my heart still races when I'm around him. And I think about him more than I want to admit. And I

132

hate that. I hate that about myself."

Lino puts his arm around Renzi and draws her to him. He rests his chin on top of her head. "Renzita, I'd tell you this love versus attraction stuff gets easier, but I'd be lying."

Renzi draws in a shuddering sigh. "I'm sorry about the flan. I can cook another one for you."

Lino grimaces. "No, nena. I'm trying to woo Julian. Not poison him."

DAVIS

I startle awake at 4:44. Something is wrong. Really wrong. Really, really, really wrong.

Severe pain-in-the-sinus wrong.

I race to the bathroom and put my finger up my nostril as I stare in the mirror. The backing of the earring-in-my-nose is not there. I knew it before I confirmed it with my pinky. And as far as I can tell, the backing is halfway up my nasal cavity, steadily making its way to my brain. I shake my head — hard — but nothing happens.

Panic starts to close in. I can feel the pressure of the backing just inches from my eyeball. I am going to die. The backing of a stupid earring stud that I am using as a nose ring is going to lodge in my brain and kill me. My obituary will label me Izzy Malone's stalker. I jump up and down, hurting and terrified.

Nothing.

I am absolutely, positively going to die. Death by inhaled earring backing.

And then, driven by instinct, I press my thumb to my unpierced nostril, shut my eyes and lips and blow as hard as I possibly can. I force air out quickly and frantically until the stud backing flies out of my nose, landing with a little ping in the sink.

I pull the stud from my nose and throw it in the garbage, my effort at radicalizing my appearance coming to a pathetic end. Maybe I'll have to shave my head. That would prove something to Izzy, show him that I have the guts that he's so convinced I lack. Shaving my head it is.

Soon.

Eventually.

I make my way to my room and fall back on my bed, my pillow still wet from hours of crying. My eyes are swollen, and my thighs ache from all the angry punches I threw at them last night.

Izzy thinks I'm a stalker and a fraud. An imposter who could never, would never, speak out for climate justice. The horrible, hateful truth about myself — Izzy found me out. He knows I'm too scared to fight for what's right. The girl who sent that letter to Premier Nancy and that tweet was a fake, not the real me. A pathetic loser of a stalker — that's the real me.

I pull my blanket over my head and draw my legs up to my chest. I know that courage is the thing I need most. There is no getting Izzy back. Maybe I don't even want that anymore. Not if he sees me as a stalker. Not if that's what I've been. Because I know it's sort of true. The endless texts. Skulking around by his locker. Sometimes walking by his house. All of that has to stop.

But I still have to prove that I can stand up for things I care about. I have to prove that I haven't been totally beaten down and forever silenced by the HateStorm. I have to show that I can and will fight to stop the tar sands and the climate change that killed Porkchop. I have to show that Izzy is wrong. I have to prove him wrong.

Starting tomorrow.

(Today, I'll just stay in bed and hide.)

JAE

Kat: I still can't believe your mom did that.
Jae: my mother is indeed pretty unbelievable.

Jae's thumbs ache from so much texting with Kat. But the soreness in her thumbs doesn't bother her. Not at all. She's been texting a lot with Jennylyn too. Making sure she's okay. Offering to write her letters of reference. Offering to keep paying her until she gets another job.

Kat: What does your dad think?
Jae: no dad. just a sperm donor.
Kat: Do you want me to talk to her? I could let
    the kat out of the bag. 😹
Jae: hells no!
Jae: but not because of you!
Jae: because of her!
Jae: she's horrible.
Jae: i don't want to expose you to that!

Shit. If her mother inadvertently ruins whatever Jae and Kat are beginning to have, this special, wonderful and totally new kind of thing, even though they haven't even kissed yet or anything, Jae will move out of her house immediately.

Not that her mother would even notice.

Jae: i haven't even introduced my mother to
renzi or davis.

Both of her friends will be so horrified when they find out that Jae's mother is the lead lawyer for Haus Oil, defending its pipeline every chance she gets. Just like they'll be horrified that Jae lives in a house that's literally an abomination of nature. They'll both feel so betrayed.

Three dots dance under Kat's name. She must be typing a long reply. Or erasing whatever she had written.

Kat: Well . . . . . .
Kat: You haven't introduced me to Renzi or Davis either.

Shit. Shit, shit and shit with a big dump of shit on top. Jae still hasn't told Renzi and Davis about Kat. Jae loves Davis a lot, and Renzi is the best friend that Jae has ever had. And Renzi's family means the world to Jae. Renzi, Lino and Marisol are forever hugging Jae, kissing her on the cheek, putting their arms around her shoulders. Jae gets more hugs from them during a single supper visit than she gets during an entire month with her mother.

An entire year, really.

Will that change when Jae introduces Kat into the equation? Will Renzi suddenly pull back or feel weird or hesitate about all the physical affection when she finds out Jae has a girlfriend? And even though Jae's brain tells her that Renzi will like Kat, her heart is maybe, possibly, just a teeny bit worried that something will shift with Renzi. That she will always insist that Kat come over for dinner too, and that this will somehow change Jae's close connection with Lino and Marisol. It's so stupid to stress about this, but the longer that Jae goes without telling Renzi about Kat, the more anxious she gets, only because she shouldn't have waited so long to tell Renzi about Kat in the first place.

But she can't let that wreck things with Kat.

Jae: i'll introduce you soon!
Jae: i promise.
Jae: please don't think i'm ashamed of you. cuz i'm not.

Three dots appear beside Kat's name again. And then they disappear. And then they reappear. And they keep flashing, sending Jae into knots of worry.

Kat: Relax, Jaebird.
Kat: You can't scare me away that easily.

Jae feels a rush of joy, a fluttery lightness that she never felt before meeting Kat, but that she now experiences almost every time they speak or text. She really wants to text a little heart emoji, but she doesn't know if she should. She isn't totally sure how Kat will react. If she'll think that's weird.

Kat: ♥

DAVIS

I slam my fingers down on the keyboard, frustrated that Izzy's cafeteria insult keeps flying through my brain. And as my fingers type the word "stalker" right in the middle of my unfinished English essay, I catch sight of the little circle above my screen. The camera.

And that is when I know exactly what to do. And how to do it.

I dig through my drawer until I find my green socks. I pull one onto my hand and draw two eyes on it with a Sharpie. It looks a lot more like a dirty green sock than a frog or even a puppet. I press record and capture just a few seconds of the sock puppet before I groan in frustration.

NEXT.

I print an image of Yoda, colour it with a green felt pen, and tape it to a pencil. It looks okay, but when I try out a Yoda voice and experiment with Yoda's mixed-up sentence structures, I admit defeat almost immediately. My dad can impersonate Yoda. I, most definitely, cannot.

NEXT.

I could probably find an old Barbie somewhere downstairs, colour her hair green and draw on some glasses. Oh my God: the one Barbie and the few stuffies I still had when we moved to Fort Mac from Calgary all got lost in the fire. How did I forget that?

NEXT.

But there is no next. I am officially out of ideas. I push my arm across my desk, shoving all my pens and papers and books to the floor. And there, peeking out from the mess at my feet, is the rectangle of sparkly green fabric that I loaned Mom the other day. The one from Red Caboose.

Yes.

I grab the scarf from the floor and tie it over my face like a bandit. I throw on my green hoodie, hiding all my hair beneath the hood. The hood and the mask transform the way I look, making my eyes brighter and hiding my de-nose-ringed nose and too-small lips. I am almost — almost — un-recognizable. I know I always look confusing to people (it's either "You look really Chinese" or "You're Chinese, really? You don't look it"), and the hoodie and scarf make me look like someone else entirely. But my voice — my throaty and gravelly and nearly-too-deep-to-be-a-girl's voice, what Ben calls my Rock Star Voice — will without question signal my identity to Izzy.

I set my computer's camera to record, making sure to look up high at the little camera instead of straight at my own image. I press record and open my mouth, only to snap it shut immediately.

I can't do this.

I did something like this with my letter and tweet — a public shaming of the tar sands — and even though the format was different, the results will no doubt be the same. And I'm not strong enough to take that chance, to risk it. I'm no GreenAída, that's for sure. I can't even say it right. Green-Eye-Eee-Da. I sound like a doofus. GreenNerd is more like it.

GreenNerd.

Yes.

"We need to talk about tar," I say, looking straight into the little round camera. That sounds awkward.

Delete.

"Let's talk about tar."

Delete.

"I survived the Fort McMurray fire, but only barely."

Delete. Delete. Delete.

I grab the book about the tar sands that I ordered online and re-read the few sections I'd highlighted. That information is what I need to communicate. I read and re-read until I know it all by heart.

"What do you get when you cut down a forest, dig up two tons of dirt and sand and pull three barrels of water from the Athabasca River?" I pause, silently counting to three for dramatic effect. "One barrel of tar sands oil."

"To get that bitumen out of the ground, oil companies use enough natural gas to heat six million homes. Every. Single. Day."

"To turn that sandy goop into something more like oil than tar, companies have to use huge amounts of energy. Just producing one barrel of tar sands oil puts three times more carbon into the air than one barrel of normal oil."

"Our Alberta tar sands use as much water each year as a city twice as big as Edmonton. And you know what happens to almost all of that water?" Pause. Don't rush it, Davis. Slow and steady for maximum impact. "Ninety percent of it ends up in these giant pools of toxic sludge called tailings ponds. And that toxic sludge leaks into the ground and poisons water. And those tailings ponds kill huge numbers of ducks and birds that land in them. That's why we need to stop this new tar sands pipeline."

I hit the pause button and then watch what I've recorded. I scribble down a script and then re-record it.

Delete.

I get the idea to set a timer to bong after a minute, a perfect closing line: "We're out of time."

Five retakes later, the GreenNerd Minute is finished.

I send the video to the only three people in the world I want to see this, with the message, "Psst . . . that's me." But I keep all their names hidden by virtue of the bcc function. Renzi and Jae don't need to know I'm sending this to Izzy too. I want to prove to him how wrong he is about me. To show him I'm not a spineless wuss. I swear it'll be the last message I ever send him.

I hope.

RENZI

"Interesting," Renzi says as she finishes rewatching the GreenNerd video Davis sent. Jae is to her left, their knees tight to their chests and their lockers cold behind their backs.

"You could call it that," Jae says. "Or you could call it hypocritical." Jae taps Renzi's purple phone case. "Made with oil." She points to the bottle of moisturizer visible behind Davis onscreen. "Oil. The energy used to make the video, to watch it, to heat our school today. Oil. Oil. Oil."

"Nena, do you work for an oil company or something? What the hell?"

Jae's eyes widen dramatically, and she looks weirdly startled. Then she shakes her head vigorously and says, "I don't disagree with what Davis is saying. The opposite, actually. Especially the part about the birds dying. It's just that if we're gonna speak out, if we're going to put ourselves out there with public protests, we need to think about counterarguments and have answers ready. And what about flying? Planes use fossil fuels, and you didn't swim to Puerto Rico over Christmas break, and I'm not walking to Toronto when I move there for university next fall."

"Carajo. You sound like my brother," Renzi groans. One law student in her life is enough, thank you very much. Every time Renzi says something about the pipeline or the tar sands at home, Lino launches into some elaborate counter-argument about how pipelines are actually better than trains and tankers, or about how new technologies are making the *oil* sands — as he always, always says — more ecologically responsible than ever. Renzi usually just responds by opening and shutting her fingers and thumb like a duck beak while voicing the words "Blah, blah, blah."

She makes the same gesture at Jae and then presses play again, listening as the masked Davis speaks about the tar sands. The production values are atrocious. Davis did nothing more than sit in front of her computer and press record, no thought to lighting or setting or sound. But Renzi can work with that. And caramba — the mask looks fabulous, the mossy colour and the sparkles making Davis's eyes and face weirdly beautiful. And her voice. *Díos mío*, that voice. Davis's voice is richer and deeper and more mesmerizing than Renzi realized.

Renzi can definitely work with this. She'll create a public YouTube channel for the video and put a link to the Green-Aída FundRazr account too. And when the money pours in, she'll be able to fund solar panel installations all over the Island, starting with her grandparents' home.

"Know what? This is more than interesting. It's brilliant. Davis should add a sign-off when that timer goes. Something like 'We're out of time. In more ways than one. This has been your GreenNerd minute.' That would be epic. And we can use more GreenNerd minutes to advertise the Die-in. To get people to come out to the protest."

Renzi taps and swipes her phone, clicking the little blue bird. GreenAída has only five Twitter followers. She taps the settings button and punches new letters in. "Goodbye, GreenAída. Hello, GreenNerd." She jumps up, shaking her head and her hips to music only she can hear.

And then she pulls Jae to her feet and kisses her on the cheek, squeezing her in a hug.

"Where do we go from here, Jae? We need to get Davis to make more of these videos and make them public. The world needs to see them. And we need to set a date for the Die-in, and a place — the Legislature steps, maybe? Or the premier's office?"

"My friend," Jae says, crossing her arms and smiling, "I'm way ahead of you on that one."

DAVIS

I'm angry at Izzy for talking shit about me.

Angry at Dad for being in Fort Mac when I most need his dorky jokes and his help with my social studies assignment.

Angry at Ben for wearing that stupid #FortMacStrong shirt again today and for not being on my side about this pipeline stuff when he's 1,000,000% on my side about absolutely everything else.

Angry at the world for not taking climate change seriously.

Furious at myself for everything. All I feel is angry, angry, angry. So I do the logical thing: I pick a fight with Mom.

The waiter sets down our dinner plates, the fresh pitas puffy with hot steam. I look at my falafel, wishing I could have justified ordering the chicken kabob (my all-time, absolute favourite).

"How can you eat that?" I ask, pointing at her beef shawarma. Righteous indignation boils up inside me. "I know you know that cow burps are full of methane. I know you

147

know that giving up meat and dairy is the best thing you can do for the planet. I know you know all of that, but here you are, letting your consumption ruin everything."

Mom looks startled, my outburst unexpected and out of character. But she recovers quickly. She always does. "Maybe my taste buds are climate change deniers." She laughs at her own joke and then puts a huge forkful of shawarma into her mouth. Mom loves Lebanese food even more than she loves Chinese food. "And if it's got four legs, and it's not a table," she says, "I will happily eat it."

"It's not funny, Mom. It's my future, not yours. I'm the one who is going to live through all the fires and droughts and floods. I'm the one who is going to have to watch as people starve, as refugees try to escape their countries and get blocked from ours. You and Dad have the luxury of your age: you'll be dead when the worst of the disasters hit, but I won't."

Mom swallows her food. She opens her mouth to say something, but I don't give her the chance.

"I know you're not a climate change denier. Dad isn't either. You guys keep talking about looking for jobs in solar power and wind energy. You know this crisis is all real, but you just don't care enough to really change. To really look hard for those better jobs. You're so comfortable, you can be apathetic. And you know what? By working on that Haus pipeline, helping to double or triple the output of the tar sands, you're worse than a climate denier — you're a climate arsonist. As if our family hasn't lost enough to fire as it is."

That last bit is a step too far. Even if it's true. I see the hurt on Mom's face, the way her eyes lose their spark and her shoulders sink. I have to look away.

"Sorry," I mumble.

Mom sits silent and still for a long moment. Seconds that feel like an hour. Then she reaches across the table and puts her hand over mine. "Rough day?"

I shut my eyes and nod, overwhelmed by her kindness. "Rough year."

She squeezes my hand, then lifts her hand to my cheek. I rest my head in her hand, wanting her to take all of my troubles away.

"Your courage, your passion, all of that gives me hope, Davis." I know she's trying to help, trying to make me feel better. But it's not working.

"Don't you see, Mom?" I say it gently, all the rage in me drained. "I don't want you to be hopeful. I want you to be freaking out. I want you to be out on the street, screaming and yelling that our world is on fire. Because it is."

And, most of all, I want you to see how terrified I am by all that happened with the fire and the HateStorm and how I'm petrified of all the horror that is to come if you don't stop building that pipeline.

I don't say that last part out loud, though. The look of sadness on Mom's face tells me she already knows.

JAE

Jae has spent more than $26,000 in the last five days.

She spent and spent in the minutes when she wasn't texting with Kat. Jae's feelings for Kat are growing at lightspeed, but it's possible her credit card bill is growing even faster.

The bill will come to Jae's mother in about two weeks. Jae's mother is too busy to ever take Jae shopping, too rarely at home when Jae needs cash, too preoccupied with work to do anything more than give her only daughter a credit card without a limit.

And every time that bill comes, each one bigger than the last, Jae figures her mother will finally say something, finally express concern or even just plain outrage about Jae's spending. But that has yet to happen. Jae has been donating $200 each month to the Wild Earth Animal Rescue, and her mother has still not said a thing.

This month, Jae is truly outdoing herself on the spending front. By a long, long stretch. And that's worth it, but Jae has no clue what her mother will do when she sees this month's bill.

Jae stares at the old-fashioned clock in the print shop, watching as its second hand ticks around and around. Tick, tick, tick. Tick, tick, tick. Jae can't shake the feeling that her time is running out. Haus Oil will be making a final announcement about its pipeline in just ten days. If that pipeline gets built, it will mean a tripling — maybe a quadrupling — of the tar sands oil output in Fort Mac. Which will mean a tripling — maybe a quadrupling — of the tailings ponds that threaten all those ducks and geese and birds. And a big, shiny promotion and raise for Jae's mother.

There is another clock ticking in Jae's mind too. But Jae can't make out the numbers on this clock, can't know how many hours, minutes and seconds are left before everything falls apart. How much time is left before Davis wakes up to the truth that Izzy Malone is completely in love with Renzi?

And how much time before Renzi's patience with her runs out? Jae still hasn't found the right moment to tell Renzi about her mother, her McMansion, Jennylyn or even about Kat, and the longer she waits, the bigger a deal her silence becomes. She keeps trying, and she keeps fumbling because the perfect moment always gets messed up.

All Jae can do is spend, hoping that the massive outpouring of money will somehow block the gushing out of the minutes. In the past few days, she has bought:

- a professional video camera to film more of Davis's GreenNerd Minutes,
- a ton of online ads hinting about the Die-in, telling Edmonton to watch and wait for April 24,

- three hugely expensive billboard displays that will soon go live,
- and 350 cardboard tombstones for the Die-in because 350 parts per million is the safe concentration of carbon dioxide in the atmosphere; the world is over 400 parts per million and still rising. And that number will rise even faster if Haus's pipeline gets built.

Jae would have bought solar panels for Renzi's grandparents too, but she didn't know enough Spanish to contact an installation company on the Island.

The printer guy at the university makes no comment about the tombstones, asking no questions about the words on the fake gravestones.

Killed by ACIDIFIED OCEANS

Killed by HURRICANES

Killed by POISONED GROUNDWATER

Killed by FLOODS

Killed by CANCER

Killed by DROUGHT AND FAMINE

Killed by FOREST FIRES

Fried alive by CLIMATE CHANGE

Jae has spent so much time preparing the tombstone designs and choosing a print shop, that she didn't consider a much bigger issue: how to carry all of the signs out to her car. Each cardboard tombstone stretches from Jae's head to her hips, and she can only fit a dozen of them into her arms at once. But when she holds them, she can't actually see where she's going.

The printer guy ignores Jae as she struggles with the tombstones, pretending to be busy on his computer. She's pretty sure she sees him smirking, though.

And then, just like that, Jae knows whose help she wants.

Lino arrives within minutes. "You do see the hypocrisy of transporting these tombstones by car, right?" Lino's voice is light and teasing, even if his point is serious.

Jae grunts in response, partly because she's struggling not to drop the signs, partly because she has no good answer.

"I keep telling Renzi that she needs to think about supply and demand. As long as there's demand for oil," Lino pauses for effect — and to rearrange the tombstones in his arms — "there will be supply. Even if you somehow manage to stop this pipeline, which I doubt is possible, someone else is just going to supply the oil. You have to take a different path if you're going to accomplish anything."

Free advice. Jae understands right then something that her mother always says: you get exactly what you pay for.

Jae has the counter-responses ready, rapid-fire answers about how the demand isn't for dirty oil in particular; it's for energy in general. To her, the problem isn't about the pipeline itself, it's the fact that it will radically expand the size of the tar sands and the bird-killing tailings ponds. But she doesn't want to talk to Lino about the pipeline. That isn't why she called him rather than Renzi or Davis.

"Can I ask you a question?"

"You just did, Jae."

They reach Lino's car and place the first load of tombstones in his backseat. Jae squeezes her eyes shut and takes a deep breath, leaning against the car and looking upward at the bright blue sky. She can do this. She trusts Lino. And she knows he'll understand.

"Was it hard to come out to your mom?"

Lino stands beside Jae, his initial look of surprise shifting immediately into one of understanding. "Oh, amiguita. I covered my room with posters of Ricky Martin when I was in grade four." He types something into his phone and hands it to Jae: googled images of a very handsome man in fashionable clothing. "It was clear to my entire family that I was interested in more than just that papito's music. Especially when I kept those posters on my wall all through high school."

"So your mom didn't just say that it's a phase?" Jae laughs, a bitter, short burst of air. "That you were just a kid and that you'd grow out of it?"

Lino puts his arm around Jae's shoulder, pulling her into a side hug and resting his cheek on top of her head. "She did not. And I am so, so sorry that yours did. It gets better, Jae. It really, really does. Especially when you stay true to yourself."

Jae nods. She has to take her chance. "And I guess being true to myself also means coming clean about the fact that my mother isn't just dismissive, she's also rolling in oil money. The same oil that all these signs are protesting."

"Ultra rich from oil?" Lino asks.

Jae shakes her head. "*Ultra*-ultra rich from oil. Like, I-was-raised-in-a-mansion-by-a-full-time-Filipina-nanny rich."

Lino lets out a low whistle. "That's a whole different kind of coming out, Jae. But those who really love you will still care for you no matter what. You just have to trust the strength of their love."

Jae's mother is wrong. Sometimes free advice isn't all bad.

DAVIS

Three hundred and fifty tombstones will need 350 bodies.
And getting 350 Albertans out to protest a pipeline will take
a whole lot of effort — in a place where everyone works for
oil companies or for companies that help oil companies, it
would be easier to get 3,500 semi-trucks on the highway
demanding new pipelines than it would be to get one-tenth
that number to stand up against one pipeline.

My hand flies up to my head, pulled like a magnet to my
worry spot. We are taking the train to film a third GreenNerd
Die-in announcement. We've already filmed one at the End
of the World, with me balancing on the edge of the embank-
ment in my GreenNerd bandit mask. We've made another
outside the Haus office building downtown, where Jae is
insisting we stage the Die-in. I should probably tell her and
Renzi that my parents work for Haus Oil. That's probably
relevant information. I should really do that.

Soon.

But first, we have to film a third video, this one on the

steps of the Alberta Legislature.

I pinch the underside of my leg as I sit on the train seat across from Jae and Renzi. I don't want to treat Premier Nancy like the enemy. I like her too much. She is warm and real and super smart, and she really seems to care about people. That's why I wrote her the Porkchop letter last year. I was stupid enough to believe that hearing about my dog might change her mind about supporting the tar sands.

Wrong.

And now the way that Premier Nancy is fighting for this pipeline feels like a complete betrayal.

She wrote a really nice email to me after my letter. Mom said it was probably written by someone on the premier's staff, but I didn't think so. I didn't want to think so. Nancy understood. But now she is on the front page of the *Edmonton Journal*, and on the radio, and all over the news announcing a boycott of British Columbia peaches, cherries, wood and wine because their premier doesn't want the pipeline running across B.C. The second I turn eighteen, I'll stockpile B.C. wine.

"Do you think Premier Nancy really believes all the things she's saying about the pipeline?" I squeak, my normally deep voice sounding like a mouse with a noose around its throat.

"You're on a first name basis with the premier, nena? You'd use her last name if she were a guy." Renzi leans forward in her seat on the train, her eyebrows raised. She stretches out her hand and gently lifts my hand from my head.

She's right, of course. Renzi is always right. "I —"

"Don't worry, Davis. I call her Nancy too." Renzi smiles. "Even though I know I shouldn't. And I don't want to shame her or anything. I like her. I actually totally admire her. I've heard she gets death threats every day, but she refuses to back down from what she believes. If she came out against the pipeline, she'd be marched right out of the Legislature and tossed on the street. But I hate that she's acting like pipelines are this province's only hope for jobs. For money. *Por favor.* What about solar? What about wind? Alberta is probably the sunniest, windiest place in Canada, and we could easily transition to those here, but she won't even consider it."

The train chime rings, announcing our arrival at Government Centre Station. Premier Nancy gets death threats? What is wrong with people? What is wrong with this province, this world? The old guy in front of me starts cleaning his eardrum with a key, jostling the key up and down, up and down. It's hard to look away, but Renzi tugs on my elbow.

"Don't forget your GreenNerd mask!"

I run back to get it from the train seat while Renzi holds the train door open with her body. Because there is no way in hell I'd film one of these GreenNerd videos without my disguise. Though how much anonymity can a thin green cloth over my nose and mouth really provide? How much protection? I never found out who'd put that charred pork chop on my locker, just like I never found out who called our school. Was it an adult who had tracked me down? Was it a kid doing cruel kid things?

Whoever it was surely is still out there, hating me.

I follow Jae and Renzi off the train, my mind still fixed on haters and trolls. My heart is pounding so hard I can feel it. My breathing is faster, my chest tighter. These GreenNerd minutes, this Die-in, this is different from my tweet. What I am doing now is so much more than just stating a fact or making a point about climate change and fire. I am demanding action.

It completely sucks that my efforts are going to pull Mom and Dad back into the horror of the HateStorm. My tweet and the backlash made them sick with worry, caused Mom to lose all that weight. Made things awkward with their co-workers and with Carly and my aunt and uncle. What damage will I do this time? Can I possibly lose any more than I've already lost? And if the HateStorm was bad before, it will surely be meaner, nastier, crueller this time around. Jae and Renzi will get hurt by it too. These two amazing friends will get hurt because I need to prove something to Izzy.

Jae puts her hands on my shoulders, bending her knees a bit so she can look me directly in the eyes. "Are you okay, Davis?"

I blink, startled. We are standing right in front of the escalator, blocking everyone else who is trying to get on. I'd froze, not even realizing it. Terror about how the trolls will react, about how all the people who depend on those oil jobs will react, all of that, had locked my knees into place.

"Courage, Davis," Renzi shouts from halfway up the escalator. "Courage."

I nod and let Jae lead me onto the moving staircase, new black steps emerging from the ground every second. Maybe things will be different this time. Maybe people won't be so angry. Maybe I'll deal with it better.

Maybe, maybe and maybe.

And maybe I really will be okay. I haven't texted or emailed Izzy since sending him the first GreenNerd video. I haven't walked past his locker or his house. And I haven't wanted to either. Not really. So maybe I can deal with whatever is coming.

"Let's do this," I say.

RENZI

Renzi stifles a yawn, refusing to admit that she's exhausted. Refusing to concede that it's time to give up and go to bed. They need to tell people about the Die-in, otherwise no one will show up. That task is on Renzi's shoulders. Jae has done so much already: making those tombstones, writing the GreenNerd scripts, buying that awesome video camera. And Davis has been amazing. It is obvious how completely freaked out she is, how nervous she is about speaking out, but she'd fought through all that fear and done a stellar job voicing those GreenNerd calls to Stand Up and Die-in.

Davis did everything Renzi asked of her — standing on the concrete ledge at the End of the World to film a shot, heading out to the big oil refineries at the edge of the city to film (and not once complaining about the choking smell), standing on the Legislature steps and repeating her GreenNerd lines in shot after shot after shot.

Now it's up to Renzi to make sure that these GreenNerd videos are perfect. Beyond perfect. They need to be brilliant, with flawless production values, and inspiring enough to get people off of their butts and out to the Die-in.

She's spent the last four hours fighting with the editing program on her ancient computer. First, the sound wasn't right. Then the clips were too choppy. Then the lighting needed adjustment. But finally, finally, finally, all three GreenNerd videos announcing the Die-in on April 24 are ready.

Renzi clicks Command + S to save.

And then she pulls her hands from the keyboard in horror as her computer makes a sharp click and the screen turns blue and then black.

Nonononononononononononononononononono.

No.

No.

Renzi presses the on button to restart the machine. It sputters to life and then clicks loudly, the death gasp of a sickly computer.

No.

All that work! They need these GreenNerd videos. And they need them to go live tonight, otherwise, there is no way that people will come to the Die-in. Even tonight is probably too late. All that work, all that time and effort. Losing it now will all be Renzi's fault, and she can't let Davis and Jae down like that. She just can't.

And it won't be just her friends she's letting down. She'll be disappointing everyone on the Island. Renzi feels like this Die-in is the only way she can really do something meaningful to help them, to fight the climate change that has stolen so much from them. She needs to get her computer fixed NOW.

Renzi grabs her phone and starts posting desperate pleas for help. There has to be a computer genius who can help her, who will run straight to her house. On every last social media account she has, even the ones she never uses anymore, Renzi calls for a computer rescuer to come to her aid. IMMEDIATELY.

She posts and checks and posts and checks, until she hears a banging on her window. Renzi looks up from her phone, startled. And then she groans.

He *would* be the one to show up.

She shakes her head and forms her lips around the word "no."

But Izzy just keeps on banging, louder and louder. He isn't going to go away, and Renzi knows he actually does have the ability to fix her computer. He's going to major in computer science next year, after all. Knowing she might well regret it, Renzi gives in.

"I think you broke your computer on purpose, you know," the Zángano says as Renzi opens the window. "You missed me." He hoists himself into her room as soon as she steps back. She really wishes she had a bedroom on the top floor of their townhouse.

She hands Izzy her laptop and then buries her face in a book, using it to shield herself.

"The master triumphs," Izzy shouts ten minutes later when the recorded sound of Davis's voice fills the room. Renzi smiles as she looks up from her book. He's fixed her computer. He's done it.

"About time," she says as she stands up to look at the computer. "You're losing your touch."

Izzy grabs Renzi by the waist and throws her over his

shoulder, doing a victory dance around her room as she pummels his back. She can't scream or Mami and Lino will come racing in. And that is definitely not what she wants.

When the Zángano finally stops running, he lowers Renzi to the floor, close to his own body. Her heart is banging against her chest, and she has a huge desire to be even closer, her mouth on his. And she hates that. She cannot stand that she's so physically attracted to a guy she really doesn't like that much. A guy so arrogant and cocky that he refuses to back off. And she loves Davis way too much to mess around with the guy she's so hung up on. Izzy keeps his hands on Renzi's hips longer than he should, and when Renzi doesn't immediately swat them away, he leans in for a kiss. She puts her hands against his chest, pushing him away.

"Don't, Izzy. I can't."

"Sure you can." He grins and pulls her toward him, and Renzi feels a quick pulse of fear. He's way bigger, way stronger than she is. She knows Izzy wouldn't actually hurt her, wouldn't actually force his lips onto hers.

But still.

He leans in again, and Renzi has no choice but to hit him. Hard. Renzi drives her upturned wrist into his nostrils, hearing a small crunch at the moment of contact.

Izzy jumps back, probably more shocked than hurt. "GAH!" He cups his hands over his nose, wincing. "What the hell?"

"I said I can't."

Izzy shakes his head, still clutching his nose. "It's because of the stalker, isn't it?" Izzy spits, his face flushed with anger. "You won't go out with me because of some weird loyalty to Davis?"

163

Renzi narrows her eyes and tosses her hair over her shoulder. "There's nothing wrong with being loyal. Maybe you should try it sometime."

He pulls his hands away from his nose. There's no blood, so she can't have hurt him that badly. He starts to say something and then stops. And they just stand there, staring at each other. Squaring off.

A sly smile creeps onto Izzy's face. "I'm going to win you back, you know."

"No, Izzy. You're not. You never HAD me in the first place." But it's not like he'll listen; he never does.

Izzy grooves a little, nodding his head and smiling. Renzi has to stifle a scream of frustration. This is what she has always liked most and hated most about Izzy: his stubbornness, his boldness, his relentlessness. But she's scared too. Because it could destroy things with Davis, and with Jae too, because Jae would rightly take Davis's side.

Plus, Izzy's behaviour is so disrespectful.

"En serio, Izzy. There is no winning me over, winning me back, or winning me. I'm not a prize. And I'm not interested. Seriously."

"I'm gonna win your heart. Just watch me." He winks and blows a kiss, and before Renzi can say anything more, he disappears out her bedroom window. She hollers in frustration, feeling empty and sad and monumentally stupid. And ragingly hungry too.

As she heads down the hall to the kitchen, Renzi spots Mami in the living room. She has her legs on the couch, her glasses low on her nose as she reads a book balanced on her knees. She looks old: white streaks run through her black hair, and she has dark circles under her eyes. The hurricanes took their toll on Mami's looks, as well as on her heart.

Renzi doesn't need to say anything. Her mom looks up and then sets her book down. "Renzita, what's wrong? Come here, *amorcita*."

Renzi climbs onto the couch, leaning back against her mom's legs. Renzi relaxes as her mom embraces her. Mami's reverse hugs are the absolute best.

"Why are guys so stupid? Stubborn and pigheaded and arrogant and obnoxious. I seriously don't understand."

"Is this about that *papito chulo* I just saw climbing out of your bedroom window?"

Oh. Carajo.

Renzi tells her mom everything — about Izzy's relentless campaign, about how Jae loathes Izzy and about the kiss that led Izzy to dump Davis. Renzi tells her mom about Davis's struggles and her Izzy fixation, and about how Davis has quickly become incredibly important to her. And she tells her mom that there is a solid chance Jae and Davis will never forgive her if (when) they find out all that has transpired with Izzy.

Renzi's mom lets out a long sigh. "That's a fine mess."

A fine mess indeed.

"What should I do?"

Her mom sighs again and kisses Renzi on top of the head. "You have a good heart, Renzita. And you have an even better brain. Listen to both of them."

Renzi's trying. But her heart and her brain cannot seem to agree.

DAVIS

"Lino's right, you know," Jae says as she makes a right turn.

Renzi puts her fingers in her ears and shakes her head. "Jae! There is no sentence I could possibly hate more."

I am in the back seat of Jae's Tesla, my arms wrapped around my body. We've been filming GreenNerd videos all day, but our attempt to film at the spot where Haus's Trans-Provincial Pipeline will originate was a total failure. We couldn't even get past the security guard at the gate. The look on that guard's face, his icy refusal to let us through, his warning that we needed to turn around before we got in real trouble sent bile burbling up from my stomach into my throat. I slide my hand under my thigh and pinch myself as hard as I can so that I can focus on that pain and get my mind into safer territory.

No such luck.

"Seriously," Jae says. "I agree with him one thousand percent that reggaetón is *not* music. We have to change the background music in our GreenNerd videos. Check the comments, Renz. I bet you they're completely focused on that music you chose."

Renzi pulls out her phone and taps a bit on the screen. "Caramba! We're up to 449 views? How did that happen?" Renzi turns around and holds the phone out for me to see. "It's because of your chocolate caramel voice, amiguita."

I feel my neck turn red, my face grow blotchy. Renzi is just being nice. She is just saying that to make me feel better about being a super-dork in a bandit mask.

"I thought we aren't supposed to use food metaphors when talking about racialized women," Jae says, catching my eye in the rear-view mirror and winking.

Renzi punches her arm lightly in response. "Well, you tell me, what better words are there to describe Davis's voice?"

Jae taps her finger against her puckered lips. "Velvet. With silk threads. And maybe some fudge sauce." The light changes to green, and Jae pulls ahead.

They're just being nice. Just trying to make me feel good.

But why would they do that?

Because they like me. Me.

Oh.

And I like them too. A lot. And I like the way I am when I'm around them. When I was around Izzy, I was always trying to impress him, to win him over. When I'm around Jae and Renzi, I'm just me — loud and goofy and honest.

Sort of like I am when I'm around Ben.

Exactly like that, actually.

But just as I think that, there's a loud thump and a quick flash of black against the front windshield. Jae slams on the brakes and swerves to the curb. The driver behind us honks, leaning into his horn as he veers by. Jae is out of the car in an instant, running into the street. Renzi and I immediately follow.

"Nena? What the fuck?" Renzi screams. I follow Jae's pointed finger until I see what's going on: there's a crow lying on the road, struggling to lift its wing. Jae keeps trying to get to it, but there are too many cars passing by.

"Renzi, go stop the cars from that side," I order, holding out my hands to stop the oncoming traffic. As soon as it's safe, Jae runs to get the bird, scooping it up in her arms and then running back to her car. Renzi and I follow. Jae is shaking more than the crow.

"I'll drive, Jae," I say. "I have my licence. Just tell me where to go."

"There's a place called Wild Earth," she says, her voice breaking. "It's a wildlife rescue." Renzi helps Jae and the bird get into the backseat, then she looks up the address on her phone and gives me directions. I can hear Jae singing to the bird, comforting it.

"You drive like a grandmother!" Renzi shouts, even though I'm speeding.

I pull into the parking lot, and Jae jumps from the car the instant I turn it off. A girl comes out from behind the counter as we run in. She has a brush cut and a ring in her eyebrow, and even though she looks about our age — maybe a bit older — she takes control immediately. As Jae hands the crow to the girl, explaining the situation, the girl nods and keeps her hands over Jae's several seconds longer than is needed.

Jae blushes, her face turning the deep purple of a saskatoon berry.

"I better take this little guy to the back," the girl says, slowly pulling her hands away from Jae's. "I'm glad you brought him in, Jae. I'll keep you posted." And then she disappears through a door marked Staff Only.

"You two know each other," Renzi says to Jae as we head back to the car.

Jae drops her key fob and scrambles to pick it up. "What? Oh, yeah. I've seen her when she has her shifts here. Because she works here, and, um, we met when a train hit this coyote. Didn't I tell you about that? I really hope the crow's going to be okay. That was such a hard strike. But that girl who works here, she'll take good care of him. I mean, I'm sure she will."

Jae never babbles like this. It's adorable. I catch Renzi's eye, and I can see that she's fighting to keep from grinning.

Just like I am.

JAE

Jae showed up at the restaurant way too early. Nervous and on edge, she wandered down the block, running over possible conversation starters in her head. She wants to give things with her mother another shot. Kat convinced her to try. So did Jennylyn. It's only when Jae's phone warbles with a text that she realizes she's been walking for a solid fifteen minutes.

Mother: I'm on my way. Be there in ten.

Is that a command or just information? Jae never feels certain where her mother is concerned. Jae rushes back to the restaurant, out of breath and sweaty when she opens the door. The place is fancy but understated, quiet but not too quiet. She knows her mother will approve.

"I have a reservation for two," Jae says. "For Jae Schmidt."

Her mother is already at the table, sipping sparkling water and looking at her phone.

"Happy birthday," Jae says lightly, trying to keep her voice cheery. Her mom had already left the house by the time Jae got up in the morning, so this is the first time they've seen each other today. "Do you want some wine or something?"

Her mother shakes her head and puts her phone down. "I'll have to get back to the office afterward, so I'll stick with water. Good choice of restaurant, Jae."

A big smile breaks across Jae's face.

Her mom checks her watch. "We should probably order," she says. She raises her hand to alert the waiter. Before Jae can try out one of her conversation starters, her mother asks, "How are your classes going? When I spoke to your chemistry teacher at parent/teacher interviews last week, she said there's still plenty of time to really bring your grade up. Maybe I'll look into hiring a tutor. Your chem courses will be a lot more rigorous in Toronto, you know."

Heat rushes into Jae's ears and then across to her cheeks. She hates how her reddening face always gives away her emotions. "About that," she starts, but the waiter appears before she can say anything else. Jae's mother orders the blackened chicken and requests a rush order. There aren't a lot of vegan options on the menu, so Jae orders fries and a salad, trying not to get annoyed by the disapproving look on her mother's face.

"So I looked into it, and there is actually still a chance that I can go to the U of A in the fall. Their life sciences program does a rolling admission, and it might not be full yet. I'd really like to stay in Edmonton, Mom."

Jae's mother smiles. Sort of. The sides of her mouth lift up in what Jae figures is a smile. She reaches her hand across the table and pats Jae's hand lightly. "I didn't get to where I am by staying in Regina, Jae. I know it can be frightening, but you've pulled your grades up since last year, and there is no need to limit yourself. I don't want you to settle for good enough when you have the best within reach."

Shit.

Silence stretches out between them. And not a comfortable one either. Heather Schmidt's phone vibrates with a text and Jae thinks through her options as her mother types a response. Maybe she should try a different approach. Maybe she should try honesty. That's what Kat would recommend. "I've met someone," Jae says. Might as well put it all on the table. This conversation can't possibly go worse than it did back when she was thirteen.

Jae's mother nods at the waiter as he sets her meal down in front of her. She slices a too-large piece of blackened chicken and pops it into her mouth. With her mouth still full of half-chewed food, Heather Schmidt says, "If he's worth —"

"She," Jae interjects.

Heather Schmidt rolls her eyes. "If this person is worth your attention, they will wait. That's what my parents told me when I resisted going to Stanford, and they were right. Once I got to California, my priorities changed. I had so many more opportunities there and met so many people who were far more interesting than 'Joe from Saskatchewan'" — she makes air quotes with her knife and fork still in her hands — "people who helped me realize my full potential. I grew up in a farming family and look what I've become. You're far too young to base a major decision about your education on some relationship or crush."

"But —"

"It's my birthday, Jae. Could we please not have this

conversation here? But thank you for arranging this lunch. That was very thoughtful of you." Jae's mother stuffs another hunk of meat into her mouth and checks her phone again.

Jae sighs and stabs a few fries with her fork. Rolled eyes to the news of Jae's girlfriend was a better response than Jae had predicted, but her mother's complete unwillingness to consider Jae's desire to stay in Edmonton, her refusal to even discuss it, hurts. Really badly. There's no point in pushing the matter. This is not a fight she has any chance of winning. Maybe that means she has chickened out. Chickens. Those poor birds. No one really understands why chickens have every reason to be so scared all the time. But Jae does. She definitely does.

DAVIS

I see him staring at me before math. While everyone else is cramming for the exam, flipping through pages of notes in the hopes of absorbing derivative rules and the applications of integrations, Ben just looks at me, his sleepy eyes unreadable. I stick out my tongue and cross my eyes, our standard greeting, but he shakes his head and opens his binder.

He comes up to me after the test, sitting down in the just-vacated desk in front of me as the rest of the class files out for lunch. "This is you, right?" He hands me his phone, the screen showing a YouTube video of me in my GreenNerd bandit mask and hoodie. I freeze.

"Why would —"

"Your voice, Davis," Ben says flatly. "No one else sounds like you."

"You don't like the videos." It's a statement, not a question. Ben's disapproval couldn't be more obvious.

"You know that my brother works up there, Davis. He's basically supporting my whole family right now. My dad's an

174

electrician," Ben says. His voice is flat, and his jaw clenches. "Dad lost his job when oil prices crashed and my parents had to sell our house. My brother and my dad need this pipeline project. My whole family does. And these videos make the pipeline and the oil sands sound so evil, and that's not fair. There are lots of scientists and engineers working to make the oil sands cleaner and protect water and stuff. And the things I know you care about — our schools, our health care — all of that is paid for by oil. All of it, Davis. All of it. And here you are, kicking us while we're down."

Kicking us while we're down. That's exactly what Carly said to me the one and only time I saw her after the fire. Hearing the same words from Ben, my Ben, makes my throat feel swollen and my chest tight. I try to slide my hand under my leg to pinch it, but for a few long seconds, it's like my whole body is frozen, unable to move. Ben gets up without saying anything else, and I bite my lip so hard that it shakes me out of my weird trance. I head into the cafeteria in a daze, not even really registering Jae's presence at my side until she places her hand on mine, intercepting a punch to my leg. "You okay, Davis?"

I don't have time to answer. Renzi is too distracting. Arms in the air and fingers snapping, she is chair dancing when Jae and I reach the table, and she keeps on bopping and grooving even after we sit down.

"Someone's in a good mood," Jae says.

Renzi lowers her arms and taps out a beat on the table. "We've got over three thousand hits on YouTube! Our Twitter followers have exploded too. A ton of people will come out for the Die-in, and GreenNerd even has her first haters."

175

A little shot of vomit flies up into my throat. The acidic burn of bile takes me back to the HateStorm, the burned pork chop, the funeral home prank.

And the hate. The hate hate hate hate.

"There's a bunch of tweets that say they're called the oil sands. I responded to one by explaining the difference between 'they're,' 'their' and 'there.'" Renzi hands me her phone, but I wave it away. I'm finding it hard to breathe, like the insides of my mouth and my tongue are swelling.

"Oooh," Jae says, reading Renzi's phone. "This guy says we're communist job killers."

"Classy." Renzi laughs.

"What changed?" I ask, the question barely making its way out of my throat. "Why the jump in numbers and comments?"

Renzi and Jae trade looks. Like they know something I don't. But before either of them says anything, Renzi's phone buzzes. She swipes the screen, then laughs. "RigPig7 proclaims that he is going to hunt down GreenNerd, or, as he calls her, the 'cunty bitch.' Impressive. I didn't know the word cunt could be made into an adjective." Another buzz. "RealJosh made a new hashtag: #NerdHunt. Oooh, and we've got another ass fucker on our hands." Buzz. "And a decapitator too." Buzz. "Oooh! One who is going to decapitate GreenNerd and then shove her head up her ass! Creative."

"I don't understand this one," Jae says, holding up Renzi's phone to show me a picture of a charred piece of meat. A pork chop.

I have to get out of here. Now. I start running for the cafeteria doors. Someone knows who I am. Someone has linked me with GreenNerd. It isn't Ben, I am totally sure of that. It's someone hateful. Cruel. Porkchop flashes into my mind, a vision of her dying in the flames of our burning Fort McMurray home. Suffering, whimpering, wondering why I abandoned her. My body folds in half, my stomach punches its way up into my throat, and vomit explodes from my mouth just as I fly through the cafeteria doors. Another burst of puke follows, a full metre away from the closest garbage can.

I hear someone shout and someone else laugh.

And then I feel an arm across my shoulder.

Renzi. With Jae right beside her.

"I'll get you home, amiguita."

"I have to clean this," I sputter.

"No. You don't."

Renzi walks me out of our school, leading me to Jae's Tesla. Jae has a big test right after lunch, so she's given Renzi her key fob. After we've been driving for a few minutes, Renzi pulls over. She leans across me and points out the window. "Look over there, Davis. This is what changed. This is what the haters are upset about."

I follow Renzi's finger and see an electronic billboard on the other side of the road, but all it shows is an ad for a furniture store.

"Wait for it."

And then, a picture of a tailings pond. A huge pool of greasy blue and purple, black, brown and yellow ooze, with an outer rim of the forest that has yet to be cut down. Across the top, the question: WHAT IN TARNATION ARE WE DOING? STOP THE TAR SANDS. STOP THE HAUS PIPELINE. #Die-in #GreenNerd #April24.

"Isn't it rad? We were going to bring you here after school

to surprise you. Jae paid for it. There's another one by the Legislature and a third one by the university. Isn't it amazing?"

My body feels frozen, locked. But my mouth still works. "Someone called our school last year," I say flatly. "To plan a memorial. For me. I can't go through that —"

I can't go on. I open the passenger door and vomit again. My back arches as my whole body heaves.

"You can't let the bastards beat you, nena," Renzi says, her hand on my back.

It's too late. They already have.

RENZI

Renzi sets the book down on Davis's couch. She shuts her eyes and rubs her face, worrying about Davis, who is snoring upstairs.

She got Davis home from school and cut class to stay with her. She washed Davis's face with a wet cloth, helped her into pyjamas and tucked her into bed. Renzi caught a glimpse of the green and purple bruises on Davis's legs as she changed, but she didn't say anything — it wasn't the right moment — and she was pretty sure Davis didn't realize what Renzi had seen.

Renzi made Davis text her mom too. Sometimes, we just need our Mamis.

And then Renzi sat on Davis's bed, rocking her friend in her arms as Davis sobbed and talked about her dog and how her parents both worked for Haus as engineers and how she'd betrayed her cousin Carly and how even her friend Ben was mad and how scared she was of all the online haters. And offline ones too. When Davis had finally fallen asleep, Renzi tiptoed downstairs to wait for Davis's mom.

A key slides into the lock of Davis's front door, the loud click announcing someone's arrival. Davis's mom rushes inside and Renzi stands up quickly, respectfully putting one finger to her lips and pointing upstairs. "Davis is asleep," she whispers. "I'm Renzi."

"Is Davis okay? She texted that she threw up."

Oh, it goes way beyond that, *señora*. But Renzi only nods. She moves toward the door to get her shoes and leave, suddenly feeling awkward and shy — two things Renzi is highly unaccustomed to feeling.

"Would you stay just a minute?" Davis's mom asks. "I'm going to go up and check on Davis and then I'll be right back."

Renzi watches Davis's mom rush up the stairs, taking them two at a time. The woman looks nothing like her own mother, but they exude that same mama bear vibe: protectiveness, love, ferocity.

Renzi's phone buzzes with a text. It's Jae, asking how Davis is doing.

Renzi feels a flash of pity for Jae. She's never met Jae's mom, and Jae never, ever talks about her, but Renzi suspects Jae's mom would not have raced home from work and zoomed upstairs to check on her kid.

Renzi: She's sleeping
Renzi: Her legs are covered in bruises, though
Renzi: I have to say something to her mom
Jae: do. please.

"Thank you again for getting Davis home and staying," Davis's mom says when she comes back downstairs. She

180

sits down on the couch, facing Renzi. "I'm Christie, by the way. It is nice to finally meet you, Renzi. Davis has told me a lot about you and about your grandparents and cousins in Puerto Rico. Those hurricanes were so devastating. I can't imagine how hard that's been for your family."

"Thank you," Renzi says, a lump forming in her throat. Now she knows where Davis gets her kindness. "I know you lost your home too. And your dog. With the fire."

Davis's mom gives a sad smile and nods. "These are such scary times. So much weird weather, and so many people — so many of my co-workers — still denying that climate change is something we need to fix right now, instead of at some future point." She shakes her head.

"Or that Canada doesn't have to do anything until the Chinese do. Because they're the bad polluters." Renzi sees Davis's mom frown. And then Renzi realizes how her words must have sounded. "I mean the Chinese in China. That's all. I didn't mean you. I'm actually half Chinese."

Davis's mom smiles and chuckles lightly, waving her hand to dismiss Renzi's worry. "I knew what you meant."

Renzi smiles, relieved, and stands to leave. "I'm usually the one calling people out for the stupidly racist things they say, not the one saying them."

Davis's mom smiles sadly. "People don't really say much about me being Chinese, but if one more person tells me that my daughter doesn't really look Asian or offers commentary on how much cuter mixed-race kids are, I may lose my mind."

"The questions are worse," Renzi says, pulling on her coat. "What's your background?" She uses a lilting, high-pitched voice. "Where are you from?"

"No, I mean, where are you *from* from?" Davis's mom adds in the same silly voice. "I was born here in Edmonton, thank you very much. One of Davis's teachers in elementary school had the gall to ask my daughter, 'What are you?' What are you! As though my child were a thing rather than a person. We had a rather long chat with the principal about that one." Davis's mom sighs and runs a hand through her hair. "Thanks again for looking after Davis today. And for staying here until I could get home. That was very sweet of you."

"Ms. Mah—"

"Christie."

"Christie, do you know about the bruises on Davis's legs? I saw them as she was changing, and I'm worried she's maybe doing that to herself? Because of anxiety or something?" Renzi never speaks in questions. And she never speaks quietly. But here she is, doing both.

Davis's mom frowns, her eyebrows furrowing. But then she nods and smiles gently. She pushes up her own sleeve, showing Renzi a few light bruises. "Davis and I are both extremely klutzy, and we both bruise really easily. It's embarrassing sometimes, especially in shorts and T-shirt weather. But thanks so much for telling me, Renzi. It means the world to me that Davis has such a caring and concerned friend."

Renzi doesn't know quite how to respond, whether or not to push the issue. But she does know this: Davis's mom is so nice. Just like her daughter. It's hard to believe she works for Haus Oil, that she's one of the engineers building that pipeline. The alarm on Renzi's phone honks — an old car horn like the one on her abuelos' ancient station wagon —

182

and Renzi scrambles to silence it. Her shift at Red Caboose is starting soon, and she'll have to hustle to make it on time.

"Davis said you're an engineer." Renzi steps into her sneakers, puts her hand on the doorknob. "How hard would it be to power Puerto Rico with solar? My abuelos still don't have electricity at their house, and I don't see the point of spending billions to rebuild power lines and power stations that are just going to get knocked down all over again with the next storm. Couldn't they just use solar there instead?"

Davis's mom smiles, but she looks tired. "How long do you have?"

Renzi knows Davis's mom means how long does she have before she has to leave for her Red Caboose shift. But that isn't the answer Renzi wants to give.

"Ay, *señora*. Time is the one thing we don't have."

DAVIS

I begged Renzi to give me her YouTube password and then I removed all the GreenNerd videos around midnight. I can't endure another HateStorm. Ben figured out that I'm GreenNerd. And someone else has too: someone who linked GreenNerd with Porkchop. Maybe it's the same cruel person who put that charred piece of meat on my locker last year. Maybe it's a totally different person. Maybe dozens of other haters have connected GreenNerd to me and my letter and my tweet.

I'm nowhere near strong enough to deal with this. Nowhere near brave enough. And I'm way too chicken to even try to fight the tar sands. Not now, not ever.

No wonder Izzy dumped me. I'd dump me too.

Renzi and Jae will no doubt be next, realizing that I've been faking it all this time. I'm not a badass. I'm not even badassish. I'm just a jackass.

Mom and Dad can't find out what happened at school yesterday. I can't put them through all that worry again.

A flurry of texts comes in.

Ben: Heard u 😫 yesterday.
Ben: u ok?
Ben: I'm sorry if I was 2 hard on u in math.
Ben: it's just a sore point with me, with Dad being laid off
Ben: Lemme know if u need soup or something, ok?

He really is the sweetest guy ever.

"How are you feeling, honey?" Mom asks when I finally stumble into the kitchen. She is usually at work by now, but she is sitting at the kitchen table, wearing jeans and a T-shirt.

I shrug and take the can of coffee from the shelf. "I think I'll stay home," I say. My voice is weak and scratchy, my throat raw from all the puking. And all the screaming into my pillow.

"Coffee's probably not the best thing for your stomach, love," Mom says as I measure out heaping spoonful after spoonful of ground beans. In the background, the CBC morning guys babble away, and Mom turns up the radio's volume.

"Lots of responses to this morning's Talking Point about the anti-pipeline billboards," Morning Guy says as I pour water into the coffeemaker. "A text message from John: 'Another sign that our jobs don't matter to the foreign-funded Green Left.' An email from Linda: 'If GreenNerd had any courage, he'd have put his own name on that billboard. I'm sure my unemployed sons would love to tell him exactly why we need this pipeline.' Nakita texts: 'Bravo! Not all Albertans support the tar sands. I donated money to GreenNerd today, and I hope others do the same.' A text from Roy: 'This is free speech taken too far. I hope Haus sues these losers.'

Now, on to our traffic report. Greg?"

I'd planned to keep everything a secret from my parents, to protect them from all of this: the threats, the insults, the anger. But my mother has a creepy ability to know exactly when I'm hiding something.

(Also, I puke into the sink.)

Mom is behind me instantly. She runs a dishcloth under the tap and then wipes my face with her left hand. All while she holds me close, her right arm wrapped around my shoulders.

"It's not the flu, is it, love?"

I whisper, "No," and turn toward her, burying my face in her shoulder.

"I'm sure this brings up a lot of terrible memories for you, sweetheart." She kisses my head and just holds me.

When I finally pull away, wiping my eyes and nose with my sleeve, I make a decision. I can't handle this by myself. I need my mom. And Dad too, but he's in Fort Mac right now.

"It does bring up stuff," I say quietly. I sit at the kitchen table and pull my legs up onto the chair, resting my chin on my knees and staring out the window. I can't look Mom in the eye. "But it's more than just memories, Mom. I'm GreenNerd. With Jae and Renzi. Those are our billboards. And the HateStorm is happening all over again."

Mom sits up straight, her face so full of fear that I might throw up again. "What are you talking about, Davis? Those billboards would have cost thousands of dollars."

Really? That's news to me. I shrug and look down at the table. "Jae paid for them, I think. But I'm the one who made up GreenNerd. I made videos and Renzi posted them on

YouTube. The videos have me talking about climate change, the tar sands and stuff. And we've been planning for a big protest event."

Mom's eyes widen and she sits very still. "You've been sharing videos of yourself?"

I nod. "Wearing a mask," I whisper.

Mom opens her mouth, but all that comes out is a punch of air. She shakes her head. "Have you forgotten what happened after your tweet, Davis? You must have known how horrible, how cruel, people would be."

I shake my head. I have not forgotten. I will never, ever forget.

"Why would you do that to yourself again, sweetheart?" She waits for me to answer, but I only shrug.

"And you do realize that your father and I work for Haus Oil?"

I nod.

Mom lets out a long sigh. "Oh, Davis. I expected better judgement from you."

So did I.

So. Did. I.

JAE

Jae is standing outside Wild Earth. Again. All the texting with Kat is great, but Jae wants to hear Kat's voice. To see her. Sometimes when she goes to Wild Earth, Jae gets a little shy. But not today. Jae doesn't feel self-conscious at all. She feels excited and ready to take things to a new level with Kat.

Kat waves goodbye to her co-worker and steps outside. She is wearing the shirt Jae complimented last week, the one that shows her strong arms. The weather has jumped from wintery to summery overnight, and Jae has never been so grateful for sunshine.

And then Jae's phone warbles, the soft canary sound announcing a text.

And warbles again. And again. And then once more.

Izzy: Tell Renzi I'll be at the Die-in
Izzy: Tell her I'm going to get thousands to show up
Izzy: Including Nakita
Izzy: And tell her to unblock my number

Jae groans. She'd forgotten that Izzy had her phone number, preserved from the Christmas dance disaster. Jae squeezes her eyes shut and shakes her head in frustration, fighting the urge to hurl her phone into the street. Izzy Malone has interrupted her connection with Kat because Izzy Malone always ruins everything. Just like he is probably going to ruin the Die-in, when Davis is so fragile.

Jae's eyes are still shut when she feels Kat's hand on hers, gently prying Jae's phone from her fist. Kat tucks the phone into the back pocket of her snug, faded jeans.

Jae never imagined it would be possible to be jealous of a phone.

"I'll give your phone back as soon as you tell me to." Kat threads her arm through Jae's. Kat is thin and muscular and sinewy, but her skin is soft and warm. Jae's heart is pounding so hard that she can practically hear it contracting and releasing.

"What phone?"

Kat laughs, a low, throaty chuckle. It is by far the best sound Jae has ever heard.

"Come for a walk," Kat says.

There are a trillion other things that Jae needs to be doing. She needs to see Davis, who hasn't been to school in three days. She needs to finish posting flyers for the Die-in. She definitely needs to warn Renzi that Izzy will be at the protest. And she needs to study for her Spanish exam.

But she needs to spend time with Kat more than anything else.

Jae and Kat head to the river valley, walking down the steep wooden stairs that lead to the North Saskatchewan

189

river. The path is muddy with the last bits of melting snow and ice, the April sun unusually warm. On the trail, Jae trips on a loose branch and stumbles, but Kat catches her, breaking her fall. As Jae moves to pull away, Kat holds on to her waist a few seconds longer than necessary. Jae brushes a tiny bug from Kat's cheek and keeps her hand on Kat's face.

And then Kat kisses her.

It is Jae's first kiss since Izzy and the Christmas dance. Kat's lips are soft and full, her breath warm. Jae pulls Kat close, wanting more. Needing more. And more and more. But as Jae opens her mouth to Kat's, their noses collide and then their teeth crash together. Jae pulls away, blinking fast. "Sorry, Kat! I —"

But Kat only grins, her hands still on Jae's hips. "Don't apologize," Kat says. "We just need to practise more."

Their second kiss is even better than the first.

When Jae and Kat climb back up the stairs an hour later, they're holding hands. A cyclist lazily pedals past just as they reach the street.

It's Izzy.

He whistles and waves as he bikes past, giving Jae a big thumbs up.

Shit.

It's not an issue that Izzy now knows she has a girlfriend.

The problem is that Izzy and her own mother — two of Jae's least favourite people — know, while Renzi and Davis do not.

DAVIS

Bruises cover my legs. Green, purple and brown-blue splotches that bloom under my skin. Thank God gym class isn't mandatory in grade eleven. I've spent the last few days hiding in my room, beating myself up for all the stupid things I've done. Literally beating myself up. If someone else had done this to me, I could press charges. But I'm the one who did this, punching my own thighs and calves — one hit for every stupid thing I've done.

Like stalking Izzy and harassing him with unanswered texts for weeks after he dumped me.

Like composing sad texts to Carly, only to delete them before I clicked send. And then rewriting them and sending them.

Like taking down the GreenNerd videos. And then putting them back up and then taking them down again.

And putting them up. Only to remove them again.

How would Porkchop have reacted if she'd seen me spiralling out of control like this? She would have buried her face into my lap, blocking my punches with her body, staring up at me with her big, gloopy brown eyes, begging me to stop.

And she would have farted too. Just to make me laugh.

I laugh and then a sob bursts from my mouth. I don't want to feel this sadness. This pain. So I punch my legs until my hands throb from all the blows I've thrown over the past few days. This can't go on. It just can't.

The Die-in is today. Die Day. Izzy will be there; I saw him announce it on his Instagram page. I don't want to face him. Not when he thinks I'm a stalker.

Because that's what I am.

I land another punch against my thigh and pull my arm back, fist clenched and poised to strike when my phone buzzes.

Maybe it's Ben. Hopefully.

Or maybe it's Jae. She sent two weird texts late yesterday to both me and Renzi, saying we need to talk. I haven't been able to respond because I'm freaked out that the texts are about something I've done or said or ruined. Maybe she's mad that I didn't tell her my parents work for Haus, even though I confessed that to Renzi.

And then I punch my leg again. Yeah, Davis, because everything is always about you.

My phone buzzes a couple of times more, and I force myself to look at the screen.

Renzi: I'm downstairs
Renzi: Let me in
Renzi: Por favor, amiguita
Renzi: Please

I drop my arm, unclenching my hand. It's only been a few days since I last saw her, but I miss Renzi. I really, really miss her. And Jae too.

Davis: Okay.

I grab a pair of pants and scramble to change out of my pyjama shorts. I can't let Renzi see my bruises.

I can't let her see that side of me. The seriously messed up side.

I take a deep breath before I pull open the front door.

"Gracias a Díos," Renzi says when I open the door. She throws her arms around me in a tight hug. "I was starting to worry that you'd had a major breakdown or something."

I shrug and sit down beside her. "Just a minor one."

This long, strange silence stretches out between us. It isn't awkward or uncomfortable or anything. It's just weird. I'm used to Renzi talking and me listening, but now it seems like she's waiting for me to say something. The last thing I want to do is talk about me and my sucktacularness, so I change the subject by asking a question. Deflect, deflect, deflect.

"Is everything ready for the Die-in?"

Renzi shrugs and shakes her head. "Jae's being super weird. Those texts she sent us last night are seriously freaking me out." Renzi pulls out her phone, taps it a couple of times and hands it to me, even though I received the same messages.

Jae: tired of the secrets.

Jae: we need to talk.

Jae: haven ravine at 109th street. meet you there. tomorrow at 3.

"Do you know what she means?" My voice is quiet, scared. I just can't escape the worry that Jae is angry I didn't tell her my parents work for Haus.

Renzi shakes her head again and looks at her hands. She has long, graceful fingers with perfect nails — like a piano player. Or a hand model. The opposite of my thick, knobby fingers with chewed-down nails.

"I've been texting her and calling her, Davis, but she's not answering."

I nod and quiet descends again.

"I need to make a confession," Renzi finally says. "I knew about what happened with the Fort Mac fire, and about your letter to Premier Nancy. And the death threat. Word got around school last year. I knew about that stuff before I met you, and I wanted to meet you. I was even hoping you'd join that Climate Club I tried to start. I would have talked to you sooner, but the hurricanes hit and I just went into survival mode."

She pushes her purple-black curls away from her face and over her shoulder. My own plain brown hair hangs straight and lank. Everything about her is the opposite of me.

"Yeah, right."

She turns and looks at me. I can feel her eyes on me, but I can't meet her gaze. I know she's just trying to make me feel better.

"Davis, it's true. Everyone knows about that letter and your tweet. The Zángano even talked about it. And I know how brutal it is when climate change completely upends your life and destroys a place you care about. That was why —" Renzi's voice catches a little in her throat, "that's one of the reasons why I wanted to start hanging out with you."

There is no way. No way at all. The idea that Renzi had wanted to make friends with me, that she knew about me, is beyond impossible, beyond what my brain can process. "Who's Zángano?"

Renzi laughs. But it's a quiet, low kind of laugh. Bitter, maybe. "Zángano just means 'fool.' I refuse to call him by his real name, when Zángano suits him so much more. He's this guy I've always been really attracted to, even though I can't stand him sometimes. Most times, actually. We kissed once, even though I knew he was going out with another girl. And I feel so horrible about that." Renzi's voice snags in her throat. "It was a mistake, and I feel awful about it. But it happened. It was just kissing, and it was just once, but it happened. And I really like the other girl. Way, way more than I expected to."

Renzi looks like she's in agony, in actual physical pain.

"I totally get it," I say, putting my arm around her.

Renzi squeezes my hand and hangs her head. "Do you hate me?"

"What? No. No way." I can't believe that Renzi is worried about that. It's kind of amazing, actually, that she cares that much about what I think. That I matter that much to her.

"Really, amiguita? I am so sorry —"

"You have nothing to be sorry for, Renzi. I mean, cheating sucks and everything, but that doesn't make me mad at you."

"But —"

"Camilo Fuentes is all kinds of cute. And it rots that he cheated on someone to be with you, but seriously, Renz, how

195

could he resist? You're amazing. And it's not your fault that Camilo cheated. It's his."

Renzi groans. She puts her hands over her face and rubs her eyes. "Camilo. Fuentes." She groans again. "And the girl?"

"I do feel sorry for her, but she sounds kinda clueless."

Renzi squeezes her eyes shut. "Kinda."

RENZI

Renzi stares at Davis's back as they ride their bikes to meet Jae. She's stunned that Davis has agreed to come — if not to the Die-in, then, at least, to talk with Jae.

These are the last few precious minutes of their friendship. She is about to lose Davis forever. Because Jae is tired of secrets and is no doubt going to share the truth about Izzy's feelings for Renzi. What will that do to Davis?

Renzi's phone buzzes against her hip, and she pulls her phone from her pocket as she rides. She doesn't know the number, but the sender is far from unknown.

Yeah, she blocked Izzy's number. But Izzy just got another one.

587-867-5308: It's Izzy. Today we tell the world
587-867-5308: How we fight for our future
587-867-5308: And how I will fight for you
587-867-5308: Always and forever

"Carajo," Renzi says under her breath, her bike wobbling dangerously. She just catches herself from falling as Jae comes into sight, waiting and waving.

Time's up.

DAVIS

"Davis! You're alive!"

Jae runs over to us as Renzi and I climb off our bikes. She squeezes my arm and grins, looking genuinely pleased to see me. But maybe I'm projecting.

"I'm really glad you came," Jae says. And she puts her arm around my shoulder, giving me a side-hug. "I've been thinking about you constantly."

Because my parents work for Haus.

We lock our bikes and head into the ravine, down the gravel path. Cyclists zoom past us, and joggers' feet make crunching noises as they come up behind us.

I expect Renzi to press Jae, to demand an explanation for the texts, or to start teasing Jae, bugging her to come clean. But Renzi just keeps quiet — like a real friend would.

"I have some things to tell you both," Jae finally says. She wraps her arms around herself, and I can tell just how nervous she is. Whatever she has to say, it's going to be big.

Jae takes a deep breath. "First, I'm rich. Really, really

rich." She exhales sharply, like she's bracing herself for our surprise at her revelation.

Except that I'm not surprised. At all.

"Uh, yeah," Renzi says. "I've been waiting for you to say so out loud. You clearly wanted to keep that info to yourself, though. Like so many other things about your life, and I didn't want to pressure you into telling me until you were ready." Renzi looks over at me for confirmation and I wink, trying to keep from giggling at the shocked expression on Jae's face.

"You know?"

Renzi and I nod. I mean, she drives a Tesla. She paid for all those billboards, and the clothes she dropped off at Red Caboose were super expensive.

"Did Lino tell you?" Jae asks.

"You told LINO before you told ME?" Renzi launches into rapid-fire Spanish swear words.

I lean over to Jae and fake-whisper, "I guess that's a no. Maybe you should just tell us the other stuff."

"I have a girlfriend. Her name's Kat and she works at —"

"The animal rescue," Renzi says, just as I say, "Wild Earth."

Jae's mouth falls. Then she closes it. And she laughs. "Guess you know me better than I realized. On to the next confession." She takes another deep breath; her inhalation is loud and dramatic enough to silence Renzi. This one is going to be huge. I can tell. "I was mostly raised by my awesome nanny Jennylyn, who is from the Philippines, but my actual mother is —"

Dying.

In jail.

The premier.

My brain rushes to complete Jae's sentence.

We come to a bridge. The creek below is brown with foamy green bubbles. Jae leans out over it, her arms folded on the wooden railing. She hangs her head down and whispers, "Heather Schmidt. Heather Schmidt is my mother."

Quick, brain. Process this one. Who is Heather Schmidt? I clearly should know the answer. Heather Schmidt must be known to everyone, famous or infamous or something. Renzi lets out a low, loud whistle. The kind of whistle that signals astonishment. Shock, even.

"Wow, nena. Heather Schmidt. *Heather*. *Schmidt*. That's powerful news." Renzi shakes her head slowly, crossing her arms. "I have just one question."

Jae nods slowly, taking a deep breath.

"Okay, Jae. Here it comes. Who the hell is Heather Schmidt?"

Jae jerks upright and her eyes widen. She blinks rapidly and looks from Renzi to me, but I just lift my shoulders and shake my head. "I don't know who that is either."

"Heather Schmidt," Jae says, as though repeating the name would suddenly clue us in. "You know: the lawyer."

Nope. Nothing.

Jae shakes her head and pulls out her phone. She brings up a YouTube clip and holds it out for Renzi and me to watch. And there, in a yellow suit that I recognize from the bag of clothes Jae brought to the consignment store, is a woman who vaguely resembles Jae. But her words are ones I know by heart: they are the ones everyone in this province uses, from the premier down to the truck drivers and engineers.

We need pipelines, pipelines, pipelines. Pipelines that will bring jobs, jobs, jobs.

"Whoa."

"Whoa indeed, nena. Whoa indeed."

"That's my mother. In all her corporate glory. She works for Haus, no less. If you guys want to turn around and leave and never speak to me again, I'll understand."

I snort-laugh, a loud explosion of surprise and relief. "Jae, my parents work for Haus too."

Renzi puts her hands on Jae's shoulders and shakes her lightly. "Nena, are you for real? These are the 'secrets' you texted us about? You think I care at all who your mom is? Or what she does for a living? I care about *you*."

Jae blinks, her eyes opening and closing so fast that it almost hurts my head to look at her.

"Oh. Wow. Well, there are two more things," Jae finally says, shaking her head and steadying herself. She puts her phone back in her pocket and laces her arms through ours. She leads us off the main trail, and we have to unlink our arms to follow her single file down a little path. I keep circling my arms like a manic helicopter, pushing branches and bugs away. The path curves and opens to a clearing. In the middle of it all, a ginormous house rises three storeys high and spreads three house-widths wide. Glass and metal and white stone cut different angles, all glaring in the sun.

I sort of know this house. Kind of. A back-of-the-brain kind of familiarity.

"Caramba. I signed a petition about this house."

As soon as Renzi says that, I remember why I know the home. The owner exploited some loophole in city laws to build it, and there had been a lot of protest about how it would ruin the ravine and harm animals. There's no way that this could be Jae's house.

"Do *not* tell me this is your house, nena."

"Fine." Jae turns to face us, a sly smile on her face. "I won't tell you. But if you want to hear the last thing, you'd better come inside." She walks up to the massive front door, at least eight feet tall, and punches in a code. She pushes open the door and steps inside, waving us in. There is a massive stone staircase winding upward, a grand piano and an ugly painting that stretches from floor to ceiling.

"What's the last thing?" I ask.

Jae raises her eyebrows, her smile breaking into a full grin. "I made something special for the Die-in."

JAE

Jae waits until she hears Davis's seatbelt click into place.

"Shit! I almost forgot!" Jae exclaims, hoping against hope that it sounds genuine. "We need bungee cords to hang the banner. Renzi, come with me to get them, okay? Davis, can you stay in the car to warn us if my mother comes home?"

It's a thin excuse, but Jae needs a minute to talk to Renzi. Alone. She'd thought Davis would run to the bathroom or something before they left for the Die-in, but that hasn't happened. Jae has no choice left but to lie and hope Davis won't notice.

Davis just nods. She looks pale, with tinges of green, like she is about to collapse.

"This banner thing is a great idea," Davis squeaks, as Jae and Renzi hop out of the car.

And it is a good idea. Jae paid a ton of money for a rush printing job and the twelve-foot banner ended up looking even better than she had hoped. It has a giant yellow-orange sun toward the top and rows upon rows of solar panels at the bottom. And in the middle of the banner, words in royal blue:

We Need Solar Panels Not Pipelines

"Renz, I have one more thing to tell you." Jae closes the door behind them, showing Renzi the bungee cords she already has in her pocket. "Izzy's going to be there, and I think he's up to something. He's going to try something that's linked to you, but I don't know what. So maybe you and Davis —"

"Should go up on the roof with the banner. That's why you made this?"

Jae nods and Renzi gives a strangled shout of frustration, throwing her hands in the air.

"Should I just take Davis home?" Renzi asks. "Skip the Die-in altogether? I don't think Davis even wants to go."

Jae has asked herself the same thing. Over and over again. And she's come to a clear conclusion. Jae looks at Renzi, wondering if Renzi will agree with her.

"Davis needs to do this Die-in, doesn't she?" Renzi asks, a question that isn't really a question.

Jae nods, her heart full of love for Renzi. Jae knows how hard this must be, how much easier it would be for Renzi to bail on the protest and avoid any chance that Izzy will say or do something stupid. Jae pulls Renzi into a hug. "I think all three of us need this protest, for different reasons. There's no way I'm willing to let Izzy ruin this for us. Or the haters either. I went over to the building yesterday and checked it out. It's really easy to get to the roof, so I'll stay on the ground while you guys are up there, and I'll tackle the asshole if I need to."

Maybe she really will manage to keep Izzy away from Renzi at the Die-in. Maybe she will somehow prevent Davis from seeing Izzy and getting all awkward and weird and nervous.

Or maybe the whole protest will be a catastrophic failure.

On the upside, maybe a catastrophic failure would finally catch her mother's attention.

DAVIS

"Guys, I don't think I can —"

Jae and Renzi turn around in their seats and look at me, and their faces are so full of concern, so full of worry, that I don't have the heart to finish my sentence. I know they understand, and I also know that I don't want to let my new best friends down.

Because that's what they are to me. Best friends. Two girls I'd do anything for.

Even this.

Renzi squeezes my knee, and Jae hands me the four bungee cords. She holds onto the cords as I take them and winks at me. "You've got this, Davis," Jae says.

Jae nods at Renzi and then shifts her car into reverse. As she backs down her driveway, Jae starts outlining the plan. She will stay on the ground to hand out the tombstones that Kat is bringing in her truck. Kat's bringing the video camera too. Jae will film while Renzi and I throw the banner from the roof.

I squeeze my eyes shut, trying to convince myself that I can do this. I have to. This whole thing was my idea. Jae and Renzi have worked so hard to help me, and I know how much they want to stop this pipeline. I want that too. And to prove to Izzy — and to the bitch tweeters and those horrible people who called the school and charred that piece of meat — that the haters and cruelty won't keep me silent.

"So," Renzi says as we arrive at the Haus office building, unbuckling her seatbelt and turning to face me. "Decision time. Who is going to throw the banner, and who is going to block the door?"

Every cell in my body screams at me: Block the door. I can maybe, possibly, do that without totally wussing out. Maybe. Possibly. "I'll throw the banner," I squeak. Renzi's head jerks, just a tiny little bit, almost imperceptibly.

I pull my hand away from the worry patch on my head. And I push open the car door.

Here we go.

Jae leads us into the office building through a side door. She smiles and waves at the security guard, who nods and returns his gaze to his phone. The building is incredible: glass and stone and natural light. A fountain and towering wall of plants. It's like being in a mountain park. In nature.

Funny, that.

We file past the security guard and onto the elevator so easily, so smoothly, that I know — without even the teeniest shadow of a doubt — that this is a sign that something is going to go horribly wrong.

"So I'll get you guys up there, and then I'll run back down to video it." Jae leads us off the elevator at the top floor and down a winding maze of hallways. It's a Saturday, but a few people are in their offices anyway. At least I know my mom isn't one of them. At least there's that.

Jae leads us around a corner, and then Renzi and I crash into her; Jae has stopped mid-step. A different security guard is at the other end of the hallway, heading straight toward us. He is walking so fast that he looks like he is about to break into a run. He has a radio pressed up against his face and he is shaking his head.

Caught.

We are caught.

Relief and fear crash into me simultaneously. This is the end. And there is a solid chance that we are going to get in serious trouble: the guy looks angry. I see Jae's shoulders sag, and she takes a step back, like she is defeated.

I know what I have to do.

"Excuse me, sir?" I ask. "We're looking for Christie Mah's office. She's my mom, and we're supposed to be meeting her to go out for coffee. Do you know where her office is?"

The guard frowns. He shakes his head and moves his radio away from his mouth. "Sorry. No idea." And then he rushes past us, saying something about the "troublemakers on the street" into his radio.

Renzi grabs my hand. "That was awesome, nena. You saved us."

I almost feel proud.

Almost.

And then we are off, running down the hallway before

anyone else can catch us. The security guard must have been talking about the Die-in protesters. My chest feels tight, and my heart is racing. This is it. Izzy will see me at this protest. I can prove myself, finally.

"Shit, shit, shit," Jae whispers. "I didn't notice that yesterday. How did I not see that?" There is a big red sign on the door: Emergency Access Only. Alarm Will Sound.

We have to turn around. Regroup and reconsider and make a new plan. I meet Renzi's gaze, her expression unreadable. We can't do it. We can't.

"Let's do it," I say, and push open the door before I can change my mind. An alarm starts screaming, and Renzi cheers, running through the door and pulling the banner from her backpack. Jae gives us two thumbs up and turns around to run back toward the elevator.

Adrenaline pumps through me, propelling me to the roof's edge.

Renzi helps me connect the banner to pipes on the roof with the bungee cords. We work silently, quickly. I peek out over the roof's edge. Renzi looks over the edge too, then cheers and raises one fist in victory.

There are dozens of protesters gathered, all with cardboard tombstones. It's a much bigger turnout than I'd expected. But they aren't the only ones: there are a bunch of counter-demonstrators too. Thirty, maybe even forty. They hold signs that say, "I ♥ Alberta Oil & Gas" and "Oil Sands Strong." There are "Lay Some Pipe" and "Pipelines for a Better Canada."

They probably saw the same posters and social media invitations that got all our supporters here.

"I have to block the door," Renzi says. "Hope I'm strong enough, Davis." She pulls me into a quick hug as I nod. I look over the edge again. The counter-protesters are chanting, "Build, build, build the pipe." They sound prouder and stronger than I have ever felt.

One sign, though, stands out. It says #EthicalOil and has a picture of something blackened with flames coming out the top. I'm too far up to tell for sure what it is, but I think I know. I think it might be a pork chop. I can't look. I hear the scream of sirens, but I can't move. My arms are frozen, paralyzed.

"Nena," Renzi shouts, "throw it!"

I look down at the street again.

Izzy is there. He is wearing his pink feminism shirt and he has a megaphone in his hands. And even though I don't want him back anymore, even though I feel hurt and angry and ashamed that he calls me a stalker, and I probably deserve it, I want to show him that I'm still standing. Still fighting for what's right. I am not totally broken and defeated. Because if girls like Jae and Renzi love me, if they want me in their life, want me as their friend, then I am okay. I can do this. With Renzi and Jae on my side, I can face down the haters. Face down the hate.

I grab the banner and hurl it, flinging it out so that it will catch the air and swing down. As it drops, I hear cheering. And I hear boos too. And curses. Loud ones. Angry ones. Someone hollers the word "bitch." *Bitch*. And the sirens are getting louder. Closer. Angrier. I hear "bitch" screamed again. Bile flies into my mouth. I look out over the edge and see Izzy lift the megaphone to his mouth.

"RENZI," he shouts. I look behind me, worried that Renzi's in trouble. But she shakes her head, confused. I look back down at the protesters below and watch as Izzy puts his hand over his heart and returns the megaphone to his lips.

"I LOVE YOU!"

And life as I know it ends.

JAE

Jae thinks about the magpie almost every day.

It flashes into her mind whenever she sees a bird flying, or someone eating chicken or when she's angry at her mother.

At first, Jae hadn't even been sure what it was. She was walking home by herself — just ten years old because her mother insisted she was mature enough to get to and from school on her own — and Jae had seen the blob of black and white on the grass between the sidewalk and road. From afar, it definitely looked like a magpie, but as she got closer, Jae grew less certain. It was leaning at a strange angle and completely still. Too still to be a bird, and at too strange an angle to be anything other than a discarded toy.

Closer still, definitely a magpie. But dead. Frozen in place, like it had fallen dead from the sky. A few steps closer still, and the magpie blinked. And blinked again. It was staring straight at her, but the only thing that was moving was its eye.

It was injured, maybe stunned from a head-on collision with a window. Or a car. Jae's instinct was to help it, to pick it up and get it to a vet, but she was pretty sure that touching birds gave people that horrible bird flu. Why else would it be called bird flu? But she couldn't just walk away. She couldn't just leave it to die.

But she did.

She made herself look away and then walk away. But before she even reached the end of the block, she turned around and ran back. The magpie was still there, still leaning and still blinking. Still alive. And because Jae didn't know what else to do, she pulled out her phone and called her mother.

For once, her mom answered.

"You called me at the office for this?" her mother had asked. "No, Jae, of course you shouldn't touch it. Just leave it. I have a meeting. I have to go."

Jae did as her mother instructed. Two hours later, when Jae found herself back at that same spot on the sidewalk, looking for the bird but seeing only a few long, black tail feathers, Jae made a decision. She would never forget about that bird. The one she didn't help.

That magpie is the first thing Jae thinks of when bloody Izzy Malone screams out his love for Renzi. She knows it's on her to protect birds from harm, no matter how weird or strange it makes her seem. Davis is suddenly the magpie. And Jae needs to get up to the roof to see if Davis is okay. To see if Renzi is okay. There was no way they would not have heard what Izzy shouted into the megaphone.

Jae shoves the video camera into Kat's hands and starts running toward the building's front doors. But two black and white police SUVs, complete with flashing lights and sirens, come screeching to a halt in front of the Haus building. Cops jump from the cars; two run straight into the building, the others yell out orders.

"Show's over, everyone," a slim cop shouts. "Time to go home."

A bunch of the protesters have already started leaving, the sound of sirens enough to send them running. The counter-protestors whoop and jeer, thrusting their "Canada Needs Pipelines" and "Oil Means Jobs" signs in the air. A couple of the cops approach all the protesters, shaking their heads.

And then, from eight storeys above, the sound of Renzi screaming.

DAVIS

Izzy's words echo in my head. "RENZI! I LOVE YOU!"

I fall back on my bum, knocked over by the truths I'd refused to see. Renzi hadn't been talking about Camilo earlier today. And Izzy has been in love with Renzi all along. He dumped me because of her. She knew that, and Jae must have known too.

Our entire friendship is a lie, and I dragged them into this dangerous mess of a protest because of my own pathetic fixation on a guy who was never going to love me back. I plunged all of us into another HateStorm for absolutely nothing. I am even stupider and more irresponsible than I had feared.

I don't scream. I don't cry. I don't punch my legs. I can barely breathe. I just blink, my eyes opening and shutting so fast I am like a human strobe light. From behind, I hear a deep voice yelling, "Security."

I feel Renzi's hands on my shoulders, and then she's there in front of me, her eyes wide with concern. "Are you okay,

Davis? I'm so sorry, amiguita. I tried to tell you. I'm not with Izzy, I swear. And I can explain. But we have to go. The security guard is here, and the cops are coming. We might get arrested."

Blink.

I hear the crackle of a walkie-talkie, and then footsteps. From the edge of my peripheral vision, I see the security guard, along with two cops. I can hear the angry taunts of the counter-protesters below. "Let's go, girls," the female cop says.

Here's the thing, though: I can't move. At all. It's like I'm frozen from the inside out. I can't lift my arms; I can't move my legs. Nothing. I can breathe — just barely — and I can move my eyes and my eyelids, but that's about it.

"Nena," Renzi is still squatting in front of me, squeezing my hand. "I promise I'll explain. But we really have to go."

Explain what? There is nothing to explain. The reality of Renzi and Izzy is a truth so ridiculously, plainly obvious that my refusal to see it would be funny if it weren't so astonishingly pathetic.

I finally see the truth. Not just the truth about Renzi and Izzy or that Jae probably knew about Renzi and Izzy all along. Those truths hurt, but it's the truth about myself that has frozen me solid. All of this GreenNerd stuff, all this Die-in stuff, has been about me trying to fool Izzy, to fool Renzi and Jae, to fool myself. To trick everyone into believing that I am a badass. Someone I'll never, ever be. Someone courageous and bold who speaks out against the tar sands pipeline, who stands up for climate justice, when all I really am is a mess of fear.

I've pulled Jae and Renzi into the eye of another Hate-Storm, into all the rage and death threats, because I was ridiculously fixated on Izzy. Renzi and Jae are going to jail because of me. I am going to jail because of me. And that will just be the start of the horror. News of our arrests will spread, and the haters and trolls will know not just my name, but Renzi and Jae's names too. Will the HateStorm go further this time, will haters act on their death threats?

And my parents? Oh, God, my mom and dad. I've plunged them back into the mess too. Mom's going to lose another twenty pounds, and then she's gonna get really sick because she's already so thin. And how many more of their colleagues and our relatives are going to start ghosting them, like Carly did to me?

I want to punch my legs, punch my chest and my arms and even my face. But I can't. Because I can't even move.

"Enough of this," the female cop says, grabbing my arm. "Let's go."

My teeth are locked together, but I am able to part my lips a bit on the left side, like a mediocre ventriloquist, and say, "I can't move."

Renzi drops onto her bum. "Then I can't either."

"Christ," the cop mutters, releasing my arm. She puts her radio to her mouth. "We've got a couple of Gandhis up here. I'm going to need help."

Excellent. Just freaking excellent. My mental collapse is being mistaken for conscientious objection. I feel my body get even tighter. My shoulders are touching my earlobes, and my crossed legs pull toward one another, like there are magnets in my knees.

"Why are your hands curling like that, Davis?" Renzi sounds scared. I shift my eyes downward to my hands. My fingers are stretched out but curled in at the top knuckle. My pinkies touch my palms, and my hands themselves are curled in toward my wrists. And I can't flatten them out. I have lost control of my body. It is utterly terrifying.

"Something's wrong with me, Renzi. I can't move." I push the words out of a tiny space at the edge of my mouth. My teeth are locked together, and I can barely even open my lips. "Something's happening to my body. Something bad."

Renzi jumps up and runs to the roof's edge before either of the cops can stop her. She screams louder than I ever could have imagined possible.

"Jae! Call 911! We need a doctor!" The woman cop lunges for Renzi, pulling her back from the edge. Renzi spins toward her and screams. "Get an ambulance! My friend is having a seizure!"

And then Renzi is back beside me, her arms around me and her body pressed against mine. "It's going to be okay, Davis. It is. I swear."

Renzi holds me, her tight embrace feels so full of care. But I still can't move. All I can do is shut my eyes and wait for something to happen.

"Space, please. I'm a physician." A commanding voice booms out behind me. And then someone kneels down in front of me. Dr. Nakita Malone. Jae is there too, right behind Nakita and right beside Renzi.

And there is someone else there too. The person I least want around.

Izzy.

"Are you able to breathe freely?" Nakita doesn't touch me. Her face is expressionless, her hands on her knees as she crouches. I focus all my attention on her, blocking Izzy, Renzi and Jae from my mind as best I can.

I try to nod, but I can't. "Yes."

"Do you have intense pain anywhere?"

"No."

"Tell me your name."

"Davis Klein-Mah."

"Alright, Davis. You're having a panic attack. Nothing more." Nakita sounds bored. Entirely unconcerned. I've wanted to meet her for so long, wanted to impress her and all I am doing is irritating her. My body curls even tighter.

"Tell your brain to relax your hands, Davis. You are fully able to do this." There is nothing urgent in Nakita's voice, nothing compassionate either. Just straightforward and authoritative.

"Go on, Davis," she says. "Relax your hands."

And it is the weirdest thing: my fingers uncurl, my hands straighten.

"Good. Now lower your shoulders." Nakita waits for my body to obey, then she continues. "Now lower your knees. Uncross your legs."

And one by one, the pieces of my body follow her instructions. She tells me to stand, and I do. She tells me to walk, and I do. I feel like a robot — no emotions, no words, just obeying the commands Nakita gives me.

As she leads me toward the exit door, the female cop blocks our path. The security guard is talking on his radio.

The male cop stands with Renzi, Jae and Izzy, his outstretched arms holding them back. When the female cop shakes her head and holds up her hands, Nakita snaps at her. "This child needs medical attention, and she is under my care as a physician. Unless you want a suspension on your hands, I advise you to get out of our way. Now."

And then Nakita opens the door.

RENZI

The hallway connecting Haus's rooftop and its elevator is way too long.

But it isn't nearly long enough.

The hallway is too long, because all Renzi wants is to reach the end and get away from Izzy and the cops marching her and Jae out of the Haus building. She just wants to be away from here.

But the hallway isn't long enough, because Izzy won't shut up and Davis is definitely still within earshot, waiting beside Nakita for the elevator.

"Renzi!" Izzy shouts, even though he is right behind her. "I got, like, seventy people to show up! I texted everyone I could think of, including Nakita. I helped hand out all the tombstones, and I did it for you. Because I love you."

Renzi struggles to contain her rage. Now would be a very good time for the cops to remind Izzy about his right to remain silent. A very good time.

Maybe it's the desperation in his voice, the pleading tone,

or maybe the cops just find the whole thing funny. Whatever the case, they don't shoo Izzy away.

"Did you hear me, Renzi? I. Love. You."

Yes, she definitely heard him. And now, she needs to find language that he'll hear too. Really hear.

"You'll have to arrest me too!" Izzy tells the cops as they all walk. "I'm not leaving you, Renz!"

One cop snorts. The other one sighs. Loudly.

"Izzy," Renzi says, struggling to keep her voice steady. She wants to scream at him, to tell him to get lost and stay lost, but she knows that won't discourage him.

"You can't deny your feelings for me, Renzi. I knew you loved me when we kissed right before Valentine's Day and you wouldn't have let me into your room last week if there wasn't something incredible between us."

Carajo. Carajo. Carajo.

Davis probably heard that. Jae most definitely did. But Renzi knows that the only thing that might get Izzy to back off is the truth.

Even if Davis and Jae hear the words Renzi needs to speak.

Renzi cuts in front of Izzy, facing him with her hands out in front of her, fingers pointed to the ceiling, gesturing STOP. She walks backward, needing to make sure he listens as they walk.

"Izzy. Listen to me. Really listen. I don't hate you, but I don't like you. At all. And I don't want to be with you. Not now, not ever. And there's nothing you can do to change that. You're harassing me, Izzy. Flat-out harassing me. Even though you fight for the right things, and you believe in the right things, you're trying to wear me down and pester me into being with you. You have to accept that I don't want to be with you. And I never will. Ever."

The smile freezes on Izzy's face. A flush of red leaps up his cheeks, but he says nothing. And Renzi knows, she knows, she has to say it again. "No texts, no emails, no calls. *En serio*, I mean it. No more visits to my house. Ever."

Renzi takes a deep breath, slows her words down. She needs to make sure Izzy hears her, even if it means admitting the full ugly truth. "I was wrong to let you kiss me when you were with Davis. I had told you I wouldn't go out with you, and I was wrong to confuse you by allowing that kiss. And I was wrong to let you into my room last week to fix my computer. Those were my mistakes. But you have to leave me alone. I don't want anything to do with you."

Renzi hears the elevator ding behind her. She turns around just in time to see Davis and Nakita step into the elevator. The look of agony on Davis's face, the way she will not meet Renzi's eyes, makes it clear. Davis heard everything that Renzi said to Izzy.

"Alright," the male cop says, holding the elevator door open with one hand and waving Renzi, Jae, Izzy and the other cop forward. "Let's go."

"Just wait for the next elevator, Izzy," Nakita says to her brother. "All of you, wait for the next one." And then she reaches forward, carefully lifts the cop's hand off the elevator door and presses a button to close the doors.

"You don't mean any of that, Renzi," Izzy protests. "You just said that because of the stalker." He motions his head toward the elevator door that just closed.

Renzi stares straight ahead, trying to control her anger.

There are cops here. Now would not be a good time to murder Izzy. "Her name is Davis," Renzi says, her voice icy. "And I love her way more than I ever even *liked* you."

A second elevator arrives and Renzi steps inside, followed by the two cops, Izzy and Jae. "I made mistakes, and I own them, Izzy. But I do not like you, and I do not want to be with you. And there is nothing you can do to change that."

Izzy opens his mouth and closes it. He shoots his arm forward, pushing open the elevator door just as it begins to close.

"Go to hell, Renzi. I am so sick of shit from chicks." He stomps out of the elevator, raising his arms above his head and lifting his two middle fingers as he leaves.

"How very feminist of you," Renzi says. If Izzy hears, he doesn't react.

She looks over at Jae, hoping that her words will at least earn her a small smile from her best friend.

No such luck. Jae stares straight ahead, stone-faced.

And the elevator doors slowly close.

DAVIS

Nakita walks me out of the Haus building, her hand on my shoulder. I have no idea how far behind us Renzi, Jae, Izzy and the cops are. Really far, I hope. I can't face Renzi and Jae, knowing that I dragged them into this mess of a protest and got them arrested. And because they both lied to me about Izzy. Does Nakita know about me stalking her brother? Does she know I organized this whole thing because I am a complete and total fraud? I hobble a bit, my body still not fully under my control.

"You can stop limping," Nakita says calmly. Her words are direct, unworried. "Your body is yours, and you can walk properly."

And just like that, my limp disappears. Nakita leads us away from the Haus office building in silence, walking so quickly I have to hustle to keep up, even though I am way taller than she is. I have no idea where she is taking me.

We turn the corner and city hall looms in front of us, its angular white walls stretching toward the sky. Nakita walks, and I follow. She opens the door to city hall and leads us to the closest bench.

She is taking me to see the mayor. I have no clue what for, or what I'll say, but just thinking about having to see the mayor makes my hands curl up again.

Nakita reaches out and touches my hands. "Relax your hands, Davis. Your body is yours and" — she smiles gently, handing me her phone — "you can't call your parents if your hands are in knots."

I shake my head, gasping for air. I know I need to call Mom; I need to tell her I'm okay. And I need to go and help Renzi and Jae by telling the police it was all my fault. And I need to apologize to everyone, over and over and over again. But I don't want to do any of those things. I just want to hide under a blanket of my shame. I am stupid and pathetic. I curl my hand into a fist and send it hurtling down toward my leg.

Nakita catches my fist before I can land the blow. "Your parents, Davis. Tell me their number, and I will call."

I pull my own phone from my pocket and hit the number for home. But I can't talk to Mom. I can't tell her what I've done. How I've triggered another HateStorm. I hand the ringing phone to Nakita and listen in silence as she introduces herself, explains what happened and tells my mom to come and get me.

I blink and hold my breath, wanting to do anything other than talk. Wanting to do anything other than exist. I feel my hands tighten into fists; my knees start to lock.

I don't want to say anything, but the words come out anyway. "Everything's lost. My dog, my friends, my cousin, our world. It's all — " I choke, a strangled sob — "all burned up. I can't go on. I just can't. It's too much."

Nakita takes my hand in hers and squeezes, lightly but firmly. "I used to work just north of Fort Mac, Davis. And I lost so many patients to cancer, so many lives taken too early, in so much pain. And I have no doubt that their suffering was caused, at least in part, because their water was impacted by tar sands operations. The rage and the anger and the sorrow paralyzed me for a long time, Davis. So did the loss. Good people, parents and kids and neighbours, killed because of greed and inertia. And an unwillingness on the part of so many people and governments to change."

She looks at me, and I can tell she sees me. Really sees me.

"But you know what I've learned, Davis? I've learned that the only cure for grief is to grieve. Those are someone else's words, but they're right. The only cure for grief is to grieve. And you have a lot to grieve. All young people do. You're losing your futures, your planet, because of things our parents and grandparents and our supposed leaders did. And the way you and your friends are fighting, it's incredible to me. But it also deeply concerns me. I want you and your brave young friends to take as much care of yourselves as you are trying to take care of our planet. I see so many teenagers, girls especially, taking all their understandable rage and fear out on themselves. Taking it out on their own bodies. I pray that you and your friends will allow yourselves the space to grieve for all that you have lost and that you can find ways, healthy ways, to process all that sadness and worry. I hope you can do that, Davis. I really hope you can."

Oh.

Wow.

JAE

The sun hurts Jae's eyes as she steps back outside; the contrast between the Haus office building's artificial light and the sunshine is jarring.

But she can still see Kat, running toward her at full speed. Kat's still holding the video camera that Jae shoved into her hands a lifetime ago.

The red-headed cop shakes her head when Kat tries to get into the police car with Jae and Renzi. Kat keeps on insisting until Jae pokes her head out of the car and tells Kat to just go home, *please.*

Izzy has vanished, but Jae can't quite relish that fact. It's hard to feel triumphant when you're being driven to a police station.

As the police SUV pulls away, driving slowly and without a siren, Jae stares straight ahead, unable to look at Renzi. The smell of industrial cleaner in the back of the car is overwhelming, and Jae cannot open the window.

They hadn't really broken any laws — trespassing, maybe

— so it isn't like there's any real risk to her future. She'd expected to feel jubilant, sticking it to Haus Oil, making her mother's company look bad, doing something to try and stop more birds from dying. But with Renzi sitting in anguish beside her, and with Davis in crisis, all Jae feels is empty, as hollow as bird bones.

Jae wants to slide her hand underneath Renzi's, to weave her fingers through those of her friend and pull her into a hug.

But Renzi lied. Lied about things with Izzy. Lies upon lies. And worse than lying, Renzi betrayed Davis. And now Davis was having some kind of breakdown, a breakdown Jae had sort of seen coming, but not really. Not like this.

And it's hard not to blame Renzi for Davis's anguish. At least in part.

"You kissed Izzy when he was with Davis." Jae says it evenly, making a statement rather than asking a question. She turns to look at Renzi, to watch her answer.

Renzi lifts her eyes to meet Jae's. She nods.

"And that's why he dumped her." Again, Jae isn't asking a question, just stating a fact. And again, Renzi nods.

Jae exhales loudly, pushing the air out through her mouth. "And he was just at your house, in your room. When we were close with Davis. When we were worrying about her mental health."

Another nod.

Then a real question, one Jae doesn't know the answer to. "Did you become friends with Davis because of Izzy?"

A pause. A long beat of silence. "Maybe. I mean, I'm not totally sure. But probably. You must hate me," Renzi finally whispers.

Jae exhales, realizing that she's been holding her breath. She looks at Renzi, a long, careful gaze. "I —" Jae starts, then stops. "I just need to process this, Renz. It's a lot."

The two girls sit in an uncomfortable silence.

"I liked him for a long time before Davis came along," Renzi says. "But I couldn't tell you. Because you hated him so much. I always figured it was because of what happened at the dance — what he must represent to you. And every time I tried to talk to you about him, you made barfing noises. You were so adamant about him, and I cared so much about what you thought, so I couldn't tell you how I felt, and I just pressed those feelings down, hiding them, and then everything ended up exploding."

Jae feels a rebuttal building in her throat. She feels defensiveness rush into her mouth. But she says nothing. She just sits with what Renzi said. And as she lets the words and their meaning settle in, Jae recognizes the truth inside Renzi's comments. Jae is partly to blame for this mess too. Jae could have talked to Davis about Izzy. She should have done that instead of placing all the responsibility on Renzi's shoulders. Jae reaches over and puts her hand on top of Renzi's and nods. "You're right," she says to Renzi. "And I'm sorry."

The police officers finally bring the car to a stop, then lead Jae and Renzi into the police station. Renzi's mom and Lino are already there. Someone else is too: Jae's mother.

Heather Schmidt is wearing a black suit and heels, a fancy silver necklace around her throat. She nods at Jae and then walks straight up to the two police officers. She pulls a piece of paper from her briefcase and sets it on the front counter.

"I am the lead counsel for Haus Oil. They will not be seeking any trespassing or nuisance charges against these girls." She says this loudly, her words so forceful that they fill the entire station.

"Let's go," Heather Schmidt says to Jae, already walking toward the station's front doors. She doesn't hug Jae or squeeze her shoulder. She just starts walking. But Jae is too stunned to care. It is hard to imagine — impossible, really. Her mom protected her. Helped her.

Jae blinks. Maybe the impossible really is happening.

"Thank you for doing this, Mom." Jae gets into her mother's car. She feels so full of relief. And hope. Or, at least, the possibility of hope. Her mom came. Her mom helped. Because she is Jae's mom. They pull out of the parking lot and cut into traffic, merging to the sound of another car's honk.

"You're my daughter. I wasn't going to let my company take action against you."

Amazing. Jae feels gratitude coursing through her. Warming her. Wrapping itself around her. "I spent a lot of money, Mom, I just wanted —"

Heather Schmidt cuts off her daughter's apology. "Do you have any idea how embarrassing it would be for me if Haus pressed charges? How much it would hurt me professionally? As for your little spending spree, that was very cute, Jae. Very cute. Your savings account is now empty — I put all the money you had in it toward the credit card bill — and I've cancelled the card. I will not allow you to humiliate me like this ever again."

And there it is: the truth. Unescapable. Unmissable.

No matter how hard Jae tries, no matter what Jae does, her mother is never going to be a Mom to her.

When Heather Schmidt stops at the next red light, Jae unbuckles her seat belt and opens the door. She needs her family right now. Her true family, her real family, is her family by choice — a family that isn't related to her at all.

"Goodbye, Mother."

DAVIS

Mom races into city hall looking frantic. She looks so freaked out, so upset, I almost have another panic attack.

"Davis! Are you okay?"

Nakita stands and introduces herself to my mother, explaining — again — that she is a physician. "Davis is going to be fine. She needs to see her family doctor to talk about her panic attack, and she needs to see a therapist. Based on what Davis has been telling me, I recommend you find one who specializes in trauma and PTSD in teenagers. Intense anxiety like Davis has been experiencing sometimes gets expressed through self-harm, so the therapist you choose should also be alert to that possibility. I know some really excellent therapists, so if you need help locating someone, just let me know."

She pulls a card from her wallet and hands it to my mom, and then she turns to me. She smiles a little, her eyes full of care. "I'll check in with you later, Davis. It was really nice to meet you."

And then she is gone.

Mom sits down on the bench and gathers me into her arms. I collapse into her. "I'm so sorry, Mom." She kisses my head and holds me. We stay like this for a long time. I don't care that the people wandering through city hall can see Mom rocking me in her arms. I just don't care. Once I've stopped crying, Mom holds my hand and leads me to our SUV.

Mom opens the door on my side, and I climb in. She is still standing there beside me, and I start to say sorry again, but she won't let me.

"I'm the one who needs to apologize, sweetheart. I know how much you've been struggling, and I haven't been there for you. Not really." She kisses the top of my head. "Your friend Renzi tried to tell me how bad things were. And I didn't listen. I couldn't. I didn't want to hear it. You're everything to me, Davis, but I haven't done nearly enough to help you. I've been like a robot since the fire. Just putting one foot in front of the next without stopping."

Mom takes a deep breath. "The worst moment of my life, sweetheart, was when that funeral home called your school. It was worse than finding out the fire had destroyed our home and that Porkchop was gone. I knew it was just a cruel joke — I knew you were okay — but it still cut straight through me. The fact that someone could threaten my baby, that someone would want to inflict so much pain and fear on our family just because you spoke out against the oil sands. That destroyed me, Davis. But I just kept on going, one day to the next." Mom's voice catches in her throat.

"I'm so sorry, Mom."

"No, love, no. You have nothing to apologize for. Nothing." She draws in a shuddering breath, then tucks a strand of my hair behind my ear. "My job in life, my entire reason for being, is to protect you. To make sure you're safe. And I've failed. I've failed. I knew things needed to change. I knew *I* needed to change, but I've been on auto-pilot, working the same job, trying to live the same life, even though the fire and all that followed changed me forever. Dad feels the same way."

Mom pulls away from me a bit and wipes her eyes. "Dad and I like our co-workers, Haus treats us really well, and we like our paycheques. But he and I both feel like we've been wearing blinders, shutting out the truths of what we're involved in and what we're doing. We know our world needs to move away from oil, and we know that the move has to happen right now — not five or ten or twenty years from now. Now. Everything is on fire, and Dad and I know we've been lighting more matches with our jobs, but it was so much easier just to keep going, keep doing what we were doing and keep wearing those blinders. It took a brave young woman to pull those blinders off."

Mom wipes her eyes again and pulls out her phone. She types something and hands her phone to me. It's a video of me dropping the banner from the Haus roof. We are at 808 views.

809.

810.

"Dad told me. I called him as I drove here. He and I have been talking through our options since we found out about your billboards and your videos," Mom says as she kisses me on the head. She wraps her arms back around me. "He's coming home on the next flight, Davis. And he's going to stay home. For good."

I let that sink in. Or I try to.

As Mom drives us home, I think hard about what Nakita said about fear and anxiety, and about how that probably explains what I've been doing to my legs. And my head. And I think about what she said about grief and loss. We lost our home in Fort Mac. We lost Porkchop. I lost my relationship with Carly, and now Mom and Dad might be leaving jobs they like — even if that loss is a choice they are making on their own.

As we pull into our garage, the idea settles inside me. I know what I want to do. I still can't work through what happened with Renzi, Izzy and Jae. I need more time with that. More space. But there is a whole other set of losses that I can begin to grieve — that I need to grieve. "Mom? Can you help me plan a funeral?"

RENZI

I talk a good game
Relentless, Courageous
But the truth is
I am TERRIFIED
the Fires, the Floods, the Droughts and the Hurricanes
are intensifying
at an apocalyptic pace
People are Already Dying
because of Climate Change
while Those in Power want us to just Keep on Shopping
I panic
but panic alone is not enough
and so I will spend my Day of Rest
Sunday
at the Legislature
because if there is no action
there will be no Future
We are almost out of time
¡BASTA!

When Renzi got home from the police station last night, she holed up in her room. She had refused to come out for supper, refused to let Mami into her room, refused to see whoever it was that rang their doorbell and came inside, talking in hushed tones to Mami and Lino. Renzi wasn't ready to talk to anyone.

She wakes to her alarm at five this Sunday morning, writes her poem and pastes it across her social media accounts. She makes a sign out of the cardboard box under her bed and she's out of the house by seven, taking the train to the Legislature.

Renzi carries her sign — SUNDAY STRIKE FOR CLIMATE — under her arm as she exits the train, walking the steep steps of Government Centre Station. She can't help but think of the last time she was here, riding the escalator up from this dank, dreary underground with her two best friends behind her. This time, though, she doesn't feel energized, she doesn't feel strong. She feels empty. Heartbroken.

She's lost Jae and Davis. Her worst nightmare has come true. Losing those two girls is every bit as devastating as she had feared. The only way she can keep going, the only way she can endure, is to fight for their future. She has no illusion that she can win Jae and Davis back, but she will do everything she can to spare them from suffering on this burning planet.

At least Jae and Davis will be there for each other. Renzi takes comfort in that.

She walks toward the steps of the Legislature, the gentle April sun warming her face as the morning gets started. The

238

sky is as blue as it is on the Island, stretching on forever, even though the air here has none of the ocean humidity and salty smells that she cherishes. She takes a seat on the grand sweep of stairs, the sandstone steps leading up to the massive dome where the province's politicians gather, making decisions about her future, squabbling like kids while actual children seem to be the only ones who grasp the scale of the climate emergency.

Renzi clutches her sign and stares at the ground. Hopefully, Davis is okay. Hopefully, Jae is okay. She hasn't had the nerve to call or text either of them.

After two hours of sitting, Renzi hears a police officer approaching. Two arrests in two days would be madness. She raises her head to greet the cop, defiant. She knows the trick is to go limp, to force them to drag her away.

It isn't a cop.

It's Lino.

He sits down beside her, holding a mug of coffee and a sign of his own. "Close your mouth, Renzita." He taps her gently under the chin, laughing at the way her jaw has dropped in shock. "You're going to catch flies with your *boca* open like that."

Renzi tries to speak, but she sputters instead, a few half-formed syllables tumbling from her mouth, tripping her tongue.

"Wow," Lino laughs. "My sister is at a loss for words. If I'd known that fighting alongside you would bring this added bonus of silence, I would have shown up long ago."

She punches him on the shoulder. Hard.

"Ouch! I thought this was supposed to be a non-violent

protest," he says, rubbing his arm. "You're going to frighten the others away."

What others?

Renzi looks at her brother, her head tilted in confusion, and then she follows his gaze. Walking toward them, all with their own cardboard signs, are Camilo Fuentes and his girlfriend. Lino's boyfriend, Julian. Davis's friend, Ben. Mami. Kat.

And Jae.

Jae.

Jae.

DAVIS

Jae is sitting in the waiting room when my appointment ends, exactly where she said she would be. Mom insisted on bringing me to and from my first four therapy sessions, but when Jae offered to bring me home from this one, Mom let me say yes.

Because I miss Jae. A lot.

"How'd it go?" Jae asks, putting her phone away. I haven't seen her since the Die-in, but we've been texting for the last few days, after I finally decided to look at my phone. It's really, really good to see her.

I shrug. "It was weird. And hard. I'm not used to talking about myself so much." It was exhausting too. We walk to the parking lot in silence, but it's a nice, comfortable kind of silence. Jae has this calming effect on me. Maybe on everyone.

"Meg — that's my therapist — and I talked about apologies today. About how it can be healing, especially if you're dwelling on stuff. Turns out I'm a dweller." I say as Jae leads me to the car. "Where's the Tesla?" I ask. Jae is unlocking the door of a rusty old Toyota, definitely not electric.

"Long story. Tell me about your conversation with Meg first," Jae says.

Once we're inside the car, I pull on my seatbelt and look out the front window. And I keep talking. "I feel like I dragged you and Renzi into the Die-in and got you arrested and all of that because I was desperately running away from memories of the HateStorm and trying to block all that out by fixating on Izzy. And I'm really sorry for that. It wasn't right of me to do that. I'm working to, like, feel my feelings and my fears instead of just punching or scratching or activisting to block them out." Activisting isn't a word, but I'm pretty sure Jae knows what I mean.

Jae turns sideways to face me, not doing up her seatbelt yet. "I don't think that you need to apologize, Davis. But thank you anyway. I had my own reasons for organizing the Die-in too. It's not like I fought Haus's pipeline only because I am terrified about climate change and outraged about all those birds dying in tailings ponds. I also did it because I was seriously pissed at my mother. And because I wanted her to pay attention to me. To notice me. But that doesn't mean I don't care about climate change."

I sit with Jae's words and then continue. "My parents and I went and talked to the police about all the threats on the GreenNerd Twitter and YouTube accounts and about what happened last year at school with the burned piece of pork and stuff. There isn't much the police can do, but I still feel better now that we told them. Less scared, I think. I hadn't really clued into how afraid I've felt since everything happened last year." I rub my hands together, but in a soothing way. Not in a painful way.

"And we're having a funeral for Porkchop. I ran straight from Porkchop's death into that letter and tweet to Premier Nancy and all the hate that came with that. And then I ran from that HateStorm straight into my Izzy fixation. And when Izzy dumped me, I raced into the GreenNerd stuff. And both Nakita and Meg the therapist" — I puff out my cheeks and then exhale — "they both say I need to stop running. I need to, like, sit still, feel all my fear and grieve. So we're having a real funeral with a service and everything. At Sandy Beach because Porkchop loved the water."

Jae makes a surprised little gasp. "Could I —" she starts, but then waits a beat, like she's thinking. "That's a really good idea, Davis. My birds died. The three that I was taking care of. They were killed. I think I should do something like a funeral too. I will." She squeezes my hand. It's like a silent thank you.

My phone buzzes.

Ben: Intergalactic season finale tonight. U up for
    snark-texting throughout?
Davis: Most definitely.

Not only am I up for it, I'm looking forward to it. For real. My heart has finally caught up with what my brain has been saying all along: Ben's the guy for me. I see that now. And I feel it too. But I'm taking things very, very slowly.

"So," Jae says quietly, "Renzi asked me to do something. And because I'm, you know, living at her house now, and because I still love her despite the whole Izzy disaster, I couldn't really say no. Actually, I didn't want to say no. I had my own big part in the mess with Izzy. A huge part. I'll tell you about it whenever or if ever you want to know. Renzi's my best friend. She's my family. And so are you." Jae hands me her phone, an image of Renzi on the screen, frozen in a video stuck on pause.

"You're living with Renzi?"

Jae nods. "Since the night of the Die-in. I showed up on her doorstep with suitcases and boxes, and her mom practically carried me inside. Renzi was so totally freaked out about what happened at the Die-in that she didn't even find out until the next day that I'd moved in. This is Lino's car. He let me borrow it because my mother took back the Tesla."

Jae points to the phone. "I told Renzi I'd offer you the video, but I also told her I wouldn't ask you to watch it. So there's absolutely no pressure or anything. I'm going to leave you here with it, and I'll be back in five minutes. Watch it or don't watch it. It's totally up to you."

She squeezes my shoulder. "I'll still adore you either way. And I'll be around for you. Literally. I'm staying here for university, not going to Toronto. That's one major upside to being completely cut off from my mother's money, I guess."

And then Jae is gone, leaving me with a tiny Renzi in my hand. This is more than I can take. I still can't believe how foolish I was, how deluded.

I punch my leg, one hard blow. I move to throw another, but I hear Meg's words in my mind. "Try treating yourself the way you treat others," she said. "You wouldn't scratch your friend's head if she were upset or afraid. And you definitely wouldn't pinch or punch your friend if she were feeling scared or overwhelmed. You'd be gentle with her. You'd be kind." I stop my arm mid-air, actually restraining my right fist with my left hand. And as I do, I bump the phone and it falls to the floor of the car.

I almost hope that the video will start playing by accident. That doesn't happen.

I have to make the decision.

So I press play, and Renzi's recorded voice flies out.

"Amiguita, I'll be quick." Renzi holds up her hand, fingers outstretched. "Just five things to say, so please keep watching." She folds down her pinky finger. "One: I screwed up. Two: I'm so, so sorry. From the bottom of my heart, I am sorry. *Lo siento, nena.*" Next, her middle finger. "I had a crush on Izzy for a long time, and I knew he liked me too. We were never together, but we kissed right before Valentine's Day, even though I knew he was going out with you. It's horrible, but I am the reason he broke up with you. That was my fault, and I should have told you the truth. Because from the moment we became friends, I have loved you like a sister, like I love Jae. And I *like* you a lot more than I ever liked Izzy. I should not have hidden the truth from you, but I was scared. I was afraid of losing you as a friend, and I was scared that I'd lose Jae, because she adores you too."

I press pause. And I make myself breathe. Renzi's words echo in my head: "I have loved you like a sister, like I love Jae." I desperately want to believe her.

And I sort of do.

I start the video again, watching as Renzi pushes down her index finger. "Four: I miss you. Five: I hope you'll forgive me. And not just for the Izzy mess either. I knew about all the hate you faced last year, but I didn't think about your trauma when I first posted your GreenNerd video to YouTube or when I read out all those hateful tweets in the cafeteria. I wasn't thinking about you, I was only thinking about our protest and how energizing it was to fight, and I see now how much my actions added to your pain and retraumatized you. And for that too, I am so sorry." Renzi exhales loudly and shakes her head a little, a smile creeping back onto her face. She taps her closed fist. "Six: We still have a pipeline to fight and a future to change."

The video ends, and Renzi's face freezes on Jae's screen. I make myself sit still, doing nothing other than repeating the chant Meg taught me. Meg told me to sit with uncomfortable feelings. She told me to pay attention to those feelings, ac-knowledging them instead of scratching my head or punching my leg or rushing to fixate on something (or someone) else.

Jae opens the car door. "Ready?"

I nod. She climbs inside and smiles. I appreciate that she doesn't immediately ask about Renzi's message. That isn't Jae's style. And I feel a rush of gratitude toward her.

"Could we go somewhere, Jae? Other than my house, I mean. There's someone I need to talk to."

"Renzi?"

"Izzy."

I am who I am, and I like who I am.

I am who I am, and I like who I am.

Meg wants me to practise saying this. To say it when I wake up in the morning, to say it into the mirror, to repeat it over and over until it feels more true than false. And she really wants me to say it whenever I feel afraid. When big feelings close in, and I want to scratch my head or pinch my thigh or punch my legs to get relief, I'm supposed to say these words in my head until the feelings get less overwhelming.

I say these words over and over in my head as Izzy comes to the front door of his house, answering his dad's bellowed call. He opens the screen door just a little, not coming outside and not inviting me in. I haven't been on his front step since the night he dumped me.

"Hey." He seems uncomfortable. I am too.

"Izzy," I take a deep breath. "I am sorry I harassed you with all the text messages and by hovering near your locker and stuff. You told me it was over between us, and I didn't accept that, and that was disrespectful. You will not hear from me again."

I'm so uncomfortable and anxious right now that it's hard to breathe, but I do, and I say the words Meg taught me. "I am who I am, and I like who I am."

Izzy stands silently, as if he's waiting for me to say something else, but I don't. He winces, like he's just eaten a lemon. "Okay." It almost sounds like a question, but not quite. And it doesn't matter. I really don't care.

Goodbye. And good riddance.

I turn and head to the car.

"How'd it go?"

"As expected. Can I ask one more favour? Could you take me to Renzi's? If she's there, I mean."

Jae sends a quick text and then starts driving. She reaches forward and turns on the radio, flipping to CBC just as the 5:00 p.m. news starts.

"In a major announcement this afternoon," the news anchor says, "the federal government declares that it will fund the Trans-Provincial Pipeline to the sum of four and a half billion dollars. A spokesperson for Haus Oil, Heather Schmidt, applauded the —"

Jae hits the power button. And we drive on in silence.

We pull up in front of Renzi's townhouse. There's no parking allowed here, so Jae hits her hazard button to let me out. "Lino wants me to pick him up at Julian's, so I'm just going to drop you off. I'll be back in, like, ten minutes. Don't be too hard on Renzi, okay? She's not as tough as she seems. And she's got a good heart."

I reach over and give Jae a tight hug. "I know."

Renzi comes to the door the instant I text her that I'm on her porch. "Nena! How did you know?" She moves to hug me but then stops, like she's holding herself back. Or like she doesn't know if I'd want her arms around me. "Or maybe you don't know. Maybe you're here for something else." She closes the front door behind her and sits down on the step, looking up at me.

I have no idea what she's talking about. But that doesn't matter. I sit down beside her and take a deep breath. And then another one. I have a really strong urge to pinch my thigh, but I just take another deep breath and silently repeat: I am who I am, and I like who I am. I'm still hurt that she kissed Izzy, and I still feel horrible that I got her arrested. But the idea of our friendship ending is way more horrifying than the prospect of working to rebuild it. "I need to apologize —" I start, right as Renzi says, "I'm so—"

We look at each other. "Oh," she says, at the exact same

moment that I say the same thing.

We laugh a little. Quietly. Awkwardly. I take another deep breath. I am who I am, and I like who I am. The sun is warm and bright in the endless blue sky. The pipeline is going ahead. The tar sands will grow. But I'll keep fighting. I'll just do it my own way. A less in-your-face way. I think maybe I'll do a GreenNerd podcast. I'll keep my name private and upload it somewhere without a comments section. No likes or dislikes.

One more deep breath. "I made a lot of bad choices as I flailed around after Izzy dumped me, and I am sorry that my actions ended up exposing you to all those haters on your Twitter account and at the protest. And I'm sorry that I got you in trouble with the police. I find haters' rage and their threats terrifying, Renzi, and I am really sorry that I brought you into that HateStorm." I feel my hand lift to my head, but I lower it to my lap. I exhale, inhale, and this time, I say the words out loud. "I am who I am, and I like who I am."

Renzi throws her arms around me, almost knocking me to the ground. "Amiguita!" she shouts. "That is fabulous! Fabulous, fabulous, fabulous. You have no idea how happy those last words make me. They're the best thing I've ever heard you say. Ever. Because I adore who you are."

I return her smile. Her massive grin. And her hug. She and I are going to be okay.

More than okay. We are going to be great.

"And nena, I have to tell you, it's actually the *second* best thing I've heard today."

Before my confusion can fully register, before I can even

ask, Renzi jumps up and pulls me to standing. "Come inside and hear the best thing."

Mom and Dad are in Renzi's front hall, putting on their shoes. Renzi's mom is there too, holding a cup of coffee. They all smile when they see me.

"What's going on? Why are you guys here?"

Dad pulls me into a hug. Mom reaches out and touches my cheek. "How was your appointment, sweetheart?"

"My question first. What are you doing here?"

"We were just about to head home to tell you." She pulls a thick yellow folder out from under her arm and hands it to me. I raise my eyebrow and open the front cover to the title page:

DAVIS SOLAR: BUSINESS PLAN

"The bank called this morning, but we wanted to wait until after your appointment to tell you. Dad and I got a loan to launch our new company. We've been talking about it for a couple of months, and we got serious over the last few weeks. We're going to hire a few electricians to work with us. Renzi suggested we ask your friend Ben's dad. And we have our first client too." Mom smiles at me, and she nods at Dad, like she wants him to have a chance to tell some of the news.

"Renzi reached out last week to see if we had suggestions about a company that could do a major solar installation in Puerto Rico," Dad explains. "And boy, did we have a suggestion for her."

I shake my head, confused. "Huh?"

"It was your GreenNerd videos," Dad says. "They led to a whole bunch of donations on Renzi's FundRazr account. Principal McNally donated. That doctor, Nakita. And a ton of other donations. It's enough to panel three homes and a community centre. Mom and I both gave Haus our notice."

"I —" the words catch in my throat. "You're calling your company 'Davis'?"

"That was Renzi's idea," Mom says, lacing her arm around Dad's waist. "We like that girl's taste in names. And friends too."

Renzi thought of me. Because she loves me.

She loves me.

Renzi links her arm through mine, and I rest my head on her shoulder. I hear a little cheer — a happy hoot — from just behind the screen door. Jae is there, with Lino.

Renzi loves me. Jae loves me.

It's true. I know it's true. And that's amazing. I smile at Mom and Dad.

"Leaving your oil jobs to start a solar company. That's pretty badass."

"That's why I asked your parents to name the company after you, nena. Jae thought it was a brilliant idea too. You're pretty inspiring, Davis." Renzi squeezes my arm. I squeeze it back, then I thread my fingers through hers.

And just like that, I know I can keep pushing for what's right, doing it in my own way, alongside the friends — and the family — who love me in all my weirdness.

I might only be badassish, but that's more than enough. It really is.

AUTHOR'S NOTE

This novel is fiction, but some of the content is inspired by real events.

Fort McMurray, Alberta, suffered a devastating wildfire in May 2016. The fire destroyed about 15% of all Fort McMurray's buildings and required the evacuation of over 80,000 people. Thanks to the amazing work of first responders, no people were killed by the fire. Many family pets, however, died in the fire.

When Canada's Green Party leader Elizabeth May, along with numerous other environmentalists, linked the Fort McMurray fire to climate change, she received vicious criticism on social media. Many accused May of exploiting the tragedy for political gain.

Puerto Rico experienced two deadly hurricanes, Irma and María, in September 2017. Hurricane María was the strongest hurricane to hit Puerto Rico in nearly 100 years and it led to the deaths of 2,975 Puerto Ricans. Hurricane María destroyed the Island's power grid, and it took about eleven months to fully restore power to Puerto Rico.

Scientists have shown that human-caused global warming increased the amount of rain that fell during Hurricane María. The United Nations' Intergovernmental Panel on Climate Change also reports that climate change intensifies extreme weather events like hurricanes.

In the novel, the wildfire and the hurricanes take place four months apart. In reality, those two events were separated by sixteen months.

The character Premier Nancy Reese is inspired by former Alberta premier Rachel Notley. The two characters have similarities, including their progressive social agendas, their comments about unicorns, their support for a pipeline between Alberta and B.C. and the death threats they received because of their carbon tax policies. Nonetheless, Premier Nancy Reese is a fictional character.

Jae's references to bird deaths linked to tar sands operations in Alberta are based on fact. I drew the numbers from various CBC news stories.

Davis's comments about the tar sands in her GreenNerd videos draw from data provided in Andrew Nikiforuk's excellent book, *Tar Sands: Dirty Oil and the Future of a Continent* (see Resources page).

Nakita Malone's description of cancer rates draws from data about Fort Chipewyan in that same book.

Climate justice activists based in Edmonton have built an extraordinary movement, drawing thousands to school strikes for climate, and stressing the connections between Indigenous rights and environmental concerns. The amazing work of the Beaver Hills Warriors, Climate Justice Edmonton, Our Time and others is inspiring and heartening.

One last thing to note: I was born in Edmonton, raised just outside the city, and I live and work in this province. I have many friends and family members who work in the oil sector. A few of them work in Fort McMurray. To me, being a proud Albertan is in no way incompatible with being deeply concerned about climate change and the grave environmental impacts of the province's tar sands.

ACKNOWLEDGEMENTS

The idea for *Badass(ish)* came to me in a New York hotel room where I sat with my sister-by-choice and two of my amazing nieces. My found family means the world to me, and I am forever grateful for the support my crew of women gives me.

My writing teacher and mentor, Tara Gilboy, helped me improve this book from its earliest moments. Thank you, Tara, for your insightful critiques and wisdom, your guidance and for always reminding me that my characters need concrete goals to strive for.

My critique partner, Nicole Martin-Iverson, made sure my jokes were in service of the plot and gave the manuscript some tough love, as did my dear friends Susan Smith and Gladys McCormick. Robyn Braun coached me through the heartaches (and headaches) of the writing life, while Shannon Stunden Bower and Josie Hendrickson gave constant, steady support. Emily Stewart was incredibly generous in sharing feedback that helped me see the book's big picture and rein in pesky flashbacks.

Ileana Rodríguez-Silva has taught me more about race and colonialism than anyone else, and I am hugely grateful for her help with this book. Ili, Solsi del Moral and Gladys McCormick regularly endure my dorky jokes, teach me and lift me up. These three have also helped me see the deep connections that tie Canada to Puerto Rico.

Wendy Atkinson has been a delight to work with and Robyn So helped me to think deeply about my characters, their motivations and their fears.

Sometime last century, Florencia Mallon urged me to spend at least an hour a day writing fiction. She modelled a path that mixed academic and creative writing, and I was so lucky to work with her.

My parents have lovingly supported my writing since my (unpublished) debut novel, *The Funny Clown*, written in grade one. I am grateful for all their love and encouragement.

My biggest thanks go to my husband, Ken. His unflagging support and calm steadiness gave me the courage to persevere with fiction writing. Our son, Theo, is a bright star in these dark times, and he is my sweet, sweet reminder that a liveable planet is always worth fighting for.

RESOURCES

The following books were helpful in writing this novel:

An Action a Day Keeps Global Capitalism Away. By Mike Hudema. Toronto: Between the Lines Press, 2004.

Global Warming and the Sweetness of Life: A Tar Sands Tale. By Matt Hern and Am Johal, with Joe Sacco. Cambridge: The MIT Press, 2018.

How To Change Everything: The Young Human's Guide to Protecting the Planet and Each Other. By Naomi Klein with Rebecca Stefoff. New York: Atheneum Books, 2021.

Mi María: Surviving the Storm. Voices from Puerto Rico. Edited by Anne Chansky and Marci Denesiuk. Chicago: Haymarket Books, 2021.

Oil's Deep State: How the Petroleum Industry Undermines Democracy and Stops Action on Global Warming — in Alberta and in Ottawa. By Kevin Taft. Toronto: James Lorimer, 2017.

Tar Sands: Dirty Oil and the Future of a Continent. By Andrew Nikiforuk. Vancouver: Greystone Books, 2010.

ABOUT THE AUTHOR

Jaymie Heilman was born in Edmonton, and she lived in Wisconsin, Peru and Nova Scotia before circling back home to Alberta. She has written two books about the history of Peru and several short stories. When she's not reading or writing books for kids and teens, she's usually gardening, biking to the library or dreaming about the ocean. She lives in Edmonton with her husband, son, and a ridiculous number of books. Visit her website at jaymieheilman.com.